Gabriela Cunninghame Graham, Robert Bontine Cunninghame Graham

Father Archangel of Scotland

And Other Essays

Gabriela Cunninghame Graham, Robert Bontine Cunninghame Graham

Father Archangel of Scotland
And Other Essays

ISBN/EAN: 9783337110888

Printed in Europe, USA, Canada, Australia, Japan

Cover: Foto ©Andreas Hilbeck / pixelio.de

More available books at **www.hansebooks.com**

Father Archangel

of

Scotland

AND OTHER ESSAYS

BY

G. & R. B. CUNNINGHAME GRAHAM

LONDON

ADAM AND CHARLES BLACK

1896

'TO THE RESPECTABLE PUBLIC'

Why the adjective 'respectable' should be applied to the public rather than 'gullible,' 'adipose,' or 'flatulent,' I am unable to determine. Taken in bulk, the public is prone to eat and drink more than is good for it, either in its corporate or individual capacity. No reasoning being will maintain that its taste in art, literature, gastronomy, or politics is worth a moment's serious consideration. Its knowledge of 'knurr and spell,' or 'numismatics' is apt to be deficient. Still I presume it is respectable if only as the final court, to which all actors, politicians, mountebanks, physicians, lawyers, writers, whether of trifling articles like these or ponderous volumes destined to repose amid the dust of libraries, come for its decision.

Let it therefore be respectable because every professor, whether of ground or lofty· tumbling, in arts, literature, sciences, or veterinary surgery, by its opinion must live and have his being.

Therefore a preface is a thing quite indispensable.

Now in these latter days your preface has fallen into considerable neglect. It may be that the public has no time to spare from the perusal of the share lists to devote to prefaces. It may be that the art, like that of chiromancy, Roman glass, Byzantine mosaics, and the proper knowledge of heraldry, venery, and other things conducive to a liberal education, has been lost. It may be that advertisements have killed the preface. Perhaps the lack of noble patrons to whom to address oneself has caused its ruin. Who in cold blood could call upon a School Board Duke for his protection? The man would be pursuing (his electors), at a meeting, or perchance passing the post-office employés in review.

Prefaces and advertisement are either compliments of one another or else sworn adversaries, I don't know which. In former times the author had to do much of his own advertisement, therefore in his preface he gave a taste of what was in his book, or, if not that, of what was in himself. To-day, no matter how bad the book may be itself, the preface is almost certain to exceed it. Which latter case, for all I know, may point the moral to this little volume.

The articles which follow were all written without reference to one another. Therefore it is not unlikely that they resemble a crowd of people at a railway junction, all rushing to and fro, without connection save only of the labels on their

luggage. Still in one thing there is a
'nexus' (not of cash), for all the articles
treat chiefly of Spain or Spanish America.
Both Spain and South America are little
written of in England. Neither of the two
are capable of being dealt with in the
modern spirit. Neither in Spain nor Spanish
America do men think, act, or look at
things—men, actions, and events—in the
way of England. Therefore they must
be wrong. Nothing can interest any one
but what he knows, and that is why so
little interests most of us. Nothing is true
to nature but the ways of Brixton, Belgravia,
Scotch provincial towns, or French Bohemia
duly emasculated. Except of course the
sorrows of ladies with too few, or else
a plethora, of husbands, or the woes of
scrofulous young men a prey to folly, drink,
or syphilis. With all these subjects neither
of the humble folk who now address you is
fit to deal ; perhaps from lack of opportunity, experience, or from want of due

imagination. And most unfortunately neither of them can command a dialect in which to wrap their platitudes, so that they must go forth to a hard world, unveiled in Irish, Welsh, Manx, Somerset, or even in that all-sufficient cloak of kailyard Scotch spoken by no one under heaven, which of late has plagued us. Perchance the unavoidable admixture of Spanish morals may serve as an excuse, and cause the writings to be sufficiently unintelligible to be appreciated. If not, but only this excuse remains, as the Spanish proverb says, ' That wheresoever dwells the heart, there also lives the speech.' *Hasta despues,*

R. B. CUNNINGHAME GRAHAM.

THANKS are due to the proprietors of the *Nineteenth Century*, the *Saturday Review*, the *World*, *Pall Mall Gazette*, and the *Daily Graphic* for permission to republish such articles as have appeared in their pages.

CONTENTS

xi

FATHER ARCHANGEL OF SCOTLAND

MEDINA DEL RIO SECO, though an interesting old Castilian town, remarkable for having been at one time a sort of Nijni-Novgorod, to-day fallen into decay, and left to shepherds to pen their flocks in at night, with all its former commerce reduced to three or four of those strange little shops full of nothing useful, and other articles which only a Spaniard can possibly want, and only he on credit, is not exactly a cheerful place to be long detained in.

After looking about the broad sandy streets, and wondering where the town ends and the country begins ; after sitting down in turn on all the cracked plaster seats in the Plaza, and sauntering into the chemists' shops, the general lounge and news mart of a Spanish town ; after having seen the diligence, with three miserable mules and an apocalyptic horse, start without passengers for nowhere, with as much noise as usually accompanies the arrival of an excursion train at Euston, one feels that the excitements of the place are exhausted, and that one must go and buy something or fall asleep.

Turning into the local curiosity shop— in the smallest town in Spain there is often an 'antiquario'—I took up one of those little volumes all so common in Spain, bound in sheepskin, lettered on the back with a pen, fastened by string loops, with little shells forming the buttons, and printed in a type as faint and dusty as that on the outside of a cigar-box. After a sharp half-hour's bargain, in which the 'antiquario' and myself exhausted much rhetoric, protested we were both going to be ruined many times, and made many well-simulated pretences of leaving one another in anger, I prevailed on him to abate his first demand of twenty dollars, dollar by

2

dollar till the little volume became mine for a peseta. I did not want the book at all, but merely wished to ' pass,' or, as the Spaniards say, ' make,' time. Distinguishing as I do, with some difficulty, a semi-Pelagian from a Neo-Platonist, and being absolutely unconcerned as to the number of angels that might (but did not) stand on the point of a needle, and seldom feeling sufficiently in the frame of mind to cope with books on spiritual matters, it was with a chastened joy I found I had purchased the life of a Capuchin friar.

Still, though matters of an ultramundane nature often leave me without enthusiasm, I have always been interested in religious enterprises pursued under disadvantageous circumstances—such, for instance, as that of the attempt to convert Jews, Scotchmen, and Mahommedans. I fancy that the faith required to pursue such enterprises, if rightly exerted, might move not only a mountain but whole chains of mountains like the Andes or Himalayas ; and the attempt to preach Catholicism in Scotland had always seemed to me one of the most desperate of these theological filibustering expeditions.

The book I had acquired with so much eloquence and a peseta treated precisely of such an adventure ; pursued, moreover, in the wilds of Aberdeenshire, and in the reign of Charles of blessed memory.

It is an erroneous opinion, held by many, that all those who have suffered for religion in Scotland have been Calvinists. That this is not the case is made manifest in the admirable and astonishing *Life of Father Archangel of Scotland*—called in the world George Leslie —by Fray Francisco de Ajofrin, Doctor of Theology, Chronicler of the Holy Province of the Capuchins of the two Castilles, Commissary of the Holy Congregation for propagating the faith in North America and the missions of Thibet ; the whole written in very choice Castillian, with the necessary licences, and published at Madrid in 1737 at the office of Antonio Fernandez. Not that this is the first time this *Admirable and Astonishing Life* has been published, for it was given to the world in Tuscan by Don Juan Bautista Rinuci, Bishop of Fermo ;

again in French, by the learned Father
Francis Beccault, and printed in Paris in
1664 ; then in Portuguese, by Fray
Cristobal Almeida, of the Order of
Augustinians, and preacher to the King
of Portugal, printed at Lisbon in 1667 ;
once again in Italian, under the title of
Il Cappucino Scozzese, in Brescia, in the
year 1736. The first notice I can find of
it, however, is by Fray Basilio de Teruel,
printed in Madrid in 1659.

Notwithstanding this wealth of editions,
it seems to me probable that not one
Scotchman in ten thousand ever so much
as heard of any one of them, and, for all
I can see, the errors of Calvin (and many
others) flourish as luxuriantly in that
country as if Father Archangel had never
lived.

My edition procured from the antiquary
in the Plaza of Medina del Rio Seco is
dedicated to the 'Most Illustrious Lord
Don Manuel Maria Pablo Antonio Arizun y
Orcasitas, Marquis of Iturbieta, etc., and
contains the usual praise of his perhaps
hypothetical virtues.

I find that George Leslie was born (no date) in Aberdon or Aberden, 'car l'un et l'autre se disent.' All historians and geographers who have written of this city, such as Bauldrand, Echard, and Moreri (though Moreri is not so reliable as the other two), unite in praising its beauty. His parents were Count James Leslie and Juana Selvia. As to Juana, I suppose that to be the Spanish for Jean ; but Selvia is, I confess, too hard for me ; but there are many things besides these, mentioned by Solomon, which to me are in the same category ; Selvia as a Scotch surname is amongst them. They were Calvinists, the dominant sect in these lugubrious and mountainous provinces. Padre Axofrin draws no comparison as Buckle has done between the religion and the configuration of the country.

His father having left the errors of his life and of Calvinism when George was eight years old, his mother determined to send him to Paris to pursue his studies ; so with a competent tutor, of much learning and experience, though a bitter Calvinist,

George starts for France. Amongst other things on his departure, she enjoins him not to let the heresies of Paptists obscure the precious jewel of his Calvinistic faith. See him, then, at eight years old, arrived with his noble following in Paris, and established in a house fit for one of his condition. Imagine him pursuing his studies, as Ajofrin says, 'like even noble youths have to do'; first in the obscure paths of grammar, then rising to the awful contemplation of the Humanities.

We have on good authority that death, and division, and marriage make barren our lives; but in George's case it was neither of these, but friendship with another boy. This most astonishing, if not admirable, specimen of a boy is pained to find George's mind obfuscated with the darkness of Calvinism. I recognised a boy in this at once. It is so like boys I have known, and if I had been blindfolded and asked who was pained about the state of George's mind in all the city of Paris, I should unhesitatingly have said—a boy. This boy, when the tutor was away, took occasion, as boys will do, to turn the conversation on religious subjects, but very cautiously (*con disimulo*). Such a portentous boy could only be of noble extraction, and his father the Count, thinking of course the occasion opportune to save a soul and mark a sheep, invites the unsuspecting George to spend his holidays with his son.

Well grounded in the Calvinistic faith as we may well imagine such a youth as George to have been, still the battle was too unequal, and little by little he falls away ; little by little he forgets his mother and her teachings, perhaps forgets with pleasure the two hours' Calvinistic sermons in a church composed of equal measures of barn and windmill.

Slowly the Romish poison filters in, and the recollections of home and remembrance of the singing at divine service, only comparable to the 'indiscriminate slaughter of multitudinous swine,' grows fainter in his ears.

Naturally, near the Count's house there lived a venerable ecclesiastic, who, by his

8

sophistry and knowledge of the Gospel, gives the last push to his tottering faith, and George becomes a Catholic ; but secretly, for the venerable priest informs him that Holy Scripture[1] says 'that it is good to conceal the sacrament of the Great King.' And who was George to set himself up against Tobit ?

The tutor, who, as we may remember, was a man of experience, begins to smell a rat, and, being troubled in his mind, determines to 'mak' sikkar,' and says George must accompany him to divine worship *à la Calvin*.

At 'Xarentan,' near Paris, was the University of the *perfidious Calvin* (el perfido Calvino), and hither the tutor was accustomed to repair when he wanted to hear the right doctrine and wile away an hour or two. George, though, with greater spirit than discretion—obviously forgetting that it is good to conceal the sacrament of the Great King—refuses to accompany him, and says somewhat rudely (for we should respect the opinions of others when we have

[1] *Tobit*, xii. 71.

no power to hand the holders of them over
to the proper authorities) that he had no
mind to go to Xarentan to listen to the
ravings of Calvin, for he was a Catholic.
Now, if we were not speaking of a grave
case of conscience, I should say that here
was a pretty kettle of fish. Argument
entirely failing as per usual, George's
mother is communicated with, who, after
running through the gamut of tears, re-
proaches, and threats, finally cuts him off
with a pound Scots, declaring that no
Catholic shall sing the mass at her lug.

Poor George, finding himself, so to
speak, 'marooned' in Paris, is glad to take
up with the father of the ingenious boy
theologian, and with him is sent to Italy to
make the grand tour. Arrived at Rome,
he meets the celebrated Father Joyeuse,
once a marshal and a peer of France, and
now a Capuchin.

Whilst the quondam disputatious theo-
logic boy, now turned a gallant, trifles away
his time at fencing-schools, at palaces, and
picture-galleries, or learns, perhaps, *l'arte
de biondeggiar i capelli* from some fair

Venetian, George, as a Scotchman, passes his time in studying metaphysics with Father Joyeuse. The shrewd ex-soldier friar sees in George a man prepared to suffer all things for the Church, and so persuades him not to try the wicked world at all (as he himself was tired of it), and George becomes a Capuchin in the well-known convent of Camerino.

Says Padre Ajofrin, 'The "navigations of America" have taught all Europe that the hardest trial the constitution of a man can bear is to pass the equinoctial line; further, in this change a man loses the heavens he has been born under. He who passes the equinoctial line of religion changes not only his heavens but his very pole-star.' This will at once commend itself, if not to the perception, at least to the attention of the careful reader. 'After this change the difference of *meum* and *tuum* is buried in the world.' I myself have even observed this phenomenon in regard to *meum* and *tuum* without any perceptible equinoctial line either in physics or religion having been passed at all.

Naturally the world, his religion, and *meum* and *tuum* being changed, the only thing left for George to change was his name, and he accordingly becomes Father Archangel, and as such I shall refer to him in future.

How the characteristics of nationality come out in any great crisis of a man's life ! A Spaniard would have become a missionary in Japan, a Frenchman an Abbé in Paris, in George's circumstances. He, as a Scotchman, naturally turns to what is most natural to him, and becomes known all over Italy as the Scotch preacher. Take notice, of course, that the modern five-percent hypocritical shop-keeping Scotchman was unknown, so that the Scotchmen of that day, mostly warriors or theologians, were as different from the modern Scots as they were from Laplanders.

All this time, though, in Aberdon his mother is having a black time (*la pena negra*) on his account, thinks George a lost soul, and, not knowing Italian, would be incapable of appreciating his sermons and therefore of consoling herself for his lapse from

Calvinism, with that keen enjoyment of
pulpit eloquence which makes Scottish life
so truly admirable. What a strange unknown land Italy must have seemed to the
good lady in Aberdon! The Pope was
there, the person she had no doubt heard
described every Sunday of her life as Antichrist, and Antichrist is such a mouth-filling
word, and seems to mean so much, as often
happens with words which really mean so
very little.

In the midst of her doubts and fears, a
gentleman fresh from the grand tour in
Italy happens to visit Aberdon and tells her
George is living in Italy, turned a Capuchin,
and settled in the Marches of Ancona.

Fancy the mother's joy! George is not
dead, only a heretic! And which of all
the mothers one knows (even a Calvinistic
mother) would not rather have her son
alive, though steeped in all the heresies of
Manichee or Gnostic, than orthodox and
dead? She has another son called Henry,
reared in the paths of strictest orthodoxy,
to whom Popery and all its works are as
the Scarlet Woman of Babylon, and to whom

a church having, as we say, *Scotice*, 'a kist of whistles' in it is more repellent than a temple of Baal Peor. Him she sends to fetch her lamb straying in the Marches of Ancona. Arrived in Italy, he seeks the court of Don Francisco de la Rovere, Duke of Urbino.

How the gawky Aberdonian youth impressed the Italians of Urbino we know not — perhaps, as the wealthy lad from Tennessee or Queensland does the Parisian to-day. His Latin, freckles, possible red hair, and cheek-bones fit for hat-pegs, his aggressive Protestantism, must all have afforded subject for mirth and wonder in the Italian court. At Urbino he meets his brother, who by this time must have become quite civilised although a Capuchin. Like true Aberdonians, they fall immediately to theological debate. 'What an agreeable spectacle this must be to God, to angels, and to men (observes our author), to see two brothers, one a Catholic, the other a Calvinist, disputing on their faiths!' This may be so, of course, but still I think it would not have

struck me in that light ; but then, as the
Spaniards say, 'there are tastes that merit
sticks.'

Victory, as in duty bound (for we do
not possess Henry's account of the debate),
inclined to the side of Archangel and against
the champion of the doctrines of *el perfido
Calvino ;* worsted in argument before the
whole court of Urbino, Henry expressed
his willingness to become a Catholic. One
thing, though, disturbs him — will he be
obliged to give up his rank and position,
and never see his mother again ?

Archangel, though, had not wasted his
time in the Convent of Camerino, and I
rather suspect that Suarez and Molina had
something to do in the preparation of those
admirable sermons for which he was so
justly admired. He at once answers,
' Having found truth does not take away
from you the joys of home, and the right
to enjoy the legitimate pleasures (golf and
curling) of Aberdeen ; riches are not
against the divine law (oh! Archangel!) ;
rather can you buy heaven with them '—
though in what manner heaven is to be

purchased, Archangel omits to inform us and Henry. Then comes the official reception into the Catholic Church, and the great banquet at the court of Urbino before Henry starts for Scotland, the Duke with his own hands, on bidding him farewell, hanging round his neck a splendid gold chain and crucifix set with Balas rubies.

Having gone out for wool and come back shorn, poor Henry must have had an unpleasant journey from Urbino back to London. Here he seems to have had some qualms, if not of conscience yet of fear. Perhaps he was uneasy when he speculated on the lengths to which a Calvinistic lioness robbed by Antichrist of both her cubs could go. So he indites a letter saying he has had good health in Italy and will soon be home. His mother, all anxiety to hear of George Archangel, was astonished, for she knew that Henry was as hardy as a wolf or Highland bull and never had an ache or pain in all his life.

However, home he had to get, and in a Dutch smack (*urca Olandesa*) he sails for Aberdeen. The mother rushes out with 'Where is George?' Henry, poor fellow, begins a sort of guide-book story of his travels, the people he has met— Duke of Urbino and nobles of the court —what a fine preacher her George is, how ladies do their hair in Venice, and generally comports himself in a manner which inclines me to believe the Italian proverb, 'Inglese Italianato diavolo Incarnato,' has some foundation in it.

All this shuffling on his part raises suspicions in his mother's mind she cannot explain. Is George dead? or is he come, and waiting in Aberdeen? Is Henry married to a daughter of Antichrist, or has he fallen amongst St. Nicholas's clerks and lost his 'siller'? So after dark she steals into his room to search his luggage and his pockets like a mother in a play to see if any unconsidered trifle, as a letter from a fair Venician, a note of hand, or undertaker's bill, is there to solve the mystery. As luck would have it, the first thing she lights upon is the gold crucifix and chain given by the Duke to Henry on his departure from Urbino.

Alarums and excursions faintly shadow forth what happened at this sight. Here was indeed the abomination of desolation spoken of (I think) by Daniel, set up in a Protestant household with a vengeance. One can but deeply sympathise with the outraged lady when the shocking sight of the counterfeit presentment, done in gold of the founder of the faith she doubtless thought she held, fell on her vision.

One wonders, with the power of pit and gallows at her disposal, that she was so mild, for after many tears and scoldings Henry is only banished to the castle of Monomusco. This time it seems to me Moreri (though, as we remember, not always to be depended on) is right in placing Monomusco two leagues from Aberdon. How admirable are the works of God ! (says Padre Axofrin)—one brother in Scotland praying for the conversion of that wild and ignorant land, and the other preaching in Italy ; for all the time Archangel preaches away as if nothing unusual had happened in his family.

The scene now shifts to Paris, where it seems either that there is a dearth of preachers or that Maria de Medici, the Queen, cannot sleep easily in church during Parisian sermons, for she sends to Italy for a new court preacher. . . . The choice falls on *il Cappuccino Scozzese*, our Archangel, and he goes to Paris, there to preach before the Queen. What he preached about, his text, and length of sermon (an important matter) we are not told, but only learn that he becomes the rage there. In fact, if the Madeleine had but been built he must have preached there every Sunday to the *plus haute gomme*.

Whilst he is in Paris gathering his laurels or the vegetable, whatever it may be folk give to preachers, Gregory the Fifteenth (the Antichrist of the day) determines on a mission to those *partes infidelium*, England and Scotland, and names Archangel head of it.

In the happy days of Charles the First, a Catholic, especially a priest or friar, was contraband in England, and to get him smuggled across the Channel took far more trouble than to-day it does to introduce a library of Tauchnitz novels.

At that time as at present, ours was the land of freedom for the man with a balance at his banker's, and all society was open to him who went to church.

To enter the enchanted island (land of the free, etc.) for a Catholic meant disguise. The greatest chance to pass the religious custom-house was in the Spanish Embassy, and, as at the present time, the Spanish Embassy, speaking 'Christian' and no other tongue always requiring an interpreter, Archangel, as possessing the English language, although filtered, as we may suppose, through the medium of Aberdeen, in that capacity accompanies it.

With some repugnance he puts on a rich velvet suit guarded with gold, a hat with plumes, and rapier ; but, says Padre Ajofrin, to appease the irritation of his conscience (nothing is mentioned of the epidermis), underneath his velvet suit he wore a shirt of horse-hair.

In his purse he had a store of gold (pieces of eight), but counted it as mud—

perhaps because he had been a friar so long
without it he had forgotten that at times it
is more useful than a breviary.

Arrived in London—the author does
not tell us where he stayed or what he did
there—he meets a Scottish cavalier. A
Scottish cavalier—how strange it sounds
to-day, when one so often sees a Scotchman, a being dressed in black broadcloth,
a sort of cross between a huckster and a
preacher! Still in those days the species
Scottish cavalier must have existed, and
one meets Archangel and tells him what is
going on in Aberdon, and, not knowing
him, of his own wicked and foolish courses,
how he has been a curse to all his friends,
and generally speaks to him as our friends
discuss us in our absence.

The cavalier tells him of his mother's
sorrow at his apostasy and of his brother's
exile to Monomusco. Wishing to see his
brother, Archangel writes to Monomusco,
and Henry, under pretence of a hunting
party, slips away and travels to London.
Meeting his brother, ruffling as a gallant in
the Spanish Embassy, and not dressed as a

friar, Henry salutes him, in a fashion that if we were not treating of Aberdonians might be called chaff, and asks him if the sword he wears is to convert their mother with.

The Spanish ambassador (perhaps Gondomar), being recalled to Paris, behaves as every Spanish ambassador did in those days, and presents Archangel with a fine Spanish horse. How they always had them, so to speak about them, to give as presents, has always been a mystery to me, when transit was so difficult.

The brothers arrange to visit Aberdeen. The night before the journey Archangel spends in prayer, and with morning (perhaps for warmth) puts on a second horsehair shirt.

On the journey, so great is his humility, or so intense his terror of the Spanish horse, that, for greater self-abasement, or to arrive more quickly at his destination, or to avoid abrasion of the cuticle, or for some other reason I cannot fathom, he walks on foot, only mounting, to save appearances, when a traveller appears upon

the road.   In twenty-two days (considered
a fast passage then) he arrives in Aberdeen,
and writes to his mother to say a gentleman
wishes to see her who has known her son
in Italy.   His mother, not knowing him,
receives him ceremoniously, and his two
brothers usher him to a room, where, notwithstanding that it is August, the cold is
so intense that a great fire is blazing.   Here
one gets a document, so to speak, that
makes one confident that the scene passes
in Aberdeen.   Exquisite wine and good
beer are served to him, but Padre Ajofrin
says nothing of that whisky for which I
feel sure Archangel's soul was longing.

At dinner in the great hall he sees
people grown old whom he remembered
young, as must also have happened to the
Prodigal Son when *he* returned from his
Marches of Ancona from amongst the
swine, and the other people he consorted
with.   What, though, strikes him to the
heart, both as a Catholic and an economist,
is to see seated at the table a heretic preacher,
and to remark that not only was the perfidious Calvinist making havoc amongst the

pease brose and the cockie-leekie, but to
learn that he received three hundred ducats
for preaching heresy. One can well see
that Archangel thought that if there was
preaching to do he could do it as well, and
perhaps at as reasonable a figure, as the son
of Belial he saw battening at his mother's
table.

Long conversations ensue between Archangel and his mother and brother, and to
the latter he gives the Spanish horse,
perhaps being secretly rather glad to get
rid of him and to be able to walk comfort-
ably on foot in his hair shirt.

One thing leads to another, till at last
his mother overhears him ask a servant
why the old pigeon-house had been removed, and, on asking him how he knew
there was a pigeon-house, perceives his
trouble, feels sure it is her son, and they
fall sobbing into each other's arms, as has
been the way of mothers and sons since the
beginning, and probably will be till the end
of the human comedy.

Naturally, there is more joy over the
son who has returned from Italy than over

the ninety and nine who have remained in the wilderness of Aberdeen, and his mother freely forgives him, for all she has done, including the cutting him off at nine or ten years old with an unnegotiable pound Scots. It is agreed that religion shall not be mentioned between them—as fatuous a bargain as for a Unionist and a Gladstonian to agree not to mention Ireland during a sea passage.

Archangel, not being able to talk religion at home, sets about preaching and converting the country-people in the vicinity of Monomusco. Notwithstanding the extreme stoniness of the soil, as one would have thought, he makes, according to Padre Axofrin, such progress that he converts more than three thousand. During his peregrinations he is astonished, as well he might be, at the climate of Aberdeen, but reflects that Scotland is to the north even of England, and that the rivers Esk and Solway and the mountains of 'Eschevoit' separate it from that country, and hence apparently the cold—for your mountain is a plaguy non-conductor of heat.

Seeing, though, is believing, and his mother, seeing the 3000 or 300 (for what is a cipher after all, as I have so often reflected in reading history, sacred and profane?), thinks there is something in Archangel's faith, and proposes a theological debate between her son and the Calvinist domestic preacher. In his double capacity of theologian and Aberdonian, naturally, the prospect of a debate delights Archangel, for he knows his power, snuffs the battle from afar, and prepares to say ha-ha amongst the syllogisms. The Calvinist does not seem to have been so confident, for he rejoins, rather pertinently as it strikes me, 'that the faith needed not always to be debated on, and that if the lady was sure of being saved what more did she require?'

Archangel's mother, though, whilst wishing to see him defeated and converted, not unnaturally wished to see her son display his learning even in a bad cause, so the debate begins.

From the outset, success inclines so strongly to Archangel, that one almost inclines to believe the whole affair a put-up

job, if we were not so sure of the absolute
bona fides of the mother. From the first,
the luckless Calvinist goes down like wheat
before a sickle, or as the moral man pro-
pounded in a Scotch sermon only to be de-
molished by the propounder. Archangel
demands on what the faith of Calvin is
grounded, and the futile Calvinist rejoins,
'On the Church of Geneva.' Archangel
sees his opening and triumphantly demands,
'Is the Church of Geneva mentioned in the
Bible?' The Calvinist (I cannot help
wishing that reporters had been present and
that we had the debate *in extenso*) in-
cautiously, as it appears to me, rejoins that
he thinks it is, and promises to find the
passage in four-and-twenty hours. This is
the first passage in this *Admirable and
Astonishing Life* which raises some doubt
in my mind as to the absolute truthfulness
of the compiler, for I have known Calvinists ignorant of the binomial theorem, or of
the principles of perspective or politeness,
but rarely one who did not know the Bible
as a stockbroker knows his share list or a
mariner his compass. However, this par-

ticular Calvinist passes the watches of the
night in fruitlessly searching the Scriptures.
Archangel, on the other hand, passes the
night in prayer — though why I cannot
imagine, as he must have known that he
had a dead sure thing without the need
of prayer. In the morning the Geneva
champion says he has not had time enough,
and that if he may get a friend . . . but
that he on his part would like to know
(here my doubts begin again) where the
Church of Rome is to be found in Holy
Writ. Archangel calls for a Bible, though
I am sure he need not have done so, as the
castle was most likely stuffed with them,
and he only had to put out his hand and
take up the first book he saw. Those of
my readers who are Calvinists, and know
their Bibles, will at once see that Archangel
finds his text in the Epistle to the Romans.
On this the somewhat inconsequent preacher
rallies, and, being worsted in Scripture
history, rejoins that in his opinion the
Church of Rome and the Scarlet Lady are
convertible terms. Archangel eventually
demolishes him by pointing to the long list

of martyrs, and asking if any one had ever
died for Calvinism. The preacher, who
seems to have been as ignorant of the
history of his sect as of the Bible, and not,
apparently, thinking Servetus good enough
to cite as a Calvinist martyr, entirely peters
out, and remains as confused as a monkey
(*corrido como una mona*).

The poor man, after being worsted in
debate, having had the mortification of seeing his patroness avow herself converted to
Catholicism, and above all having lost his
salary, flies, not to Geneva, as we might
reasonably suppose, or to St. Andrews, but
to Erastian England, where he takes service
in the household of an Anglican bishop.
After this, the whole family is converted to
Catholicism, having been able to comprehend at once the directness of the reasoning
that if one Church is mentioned in the Bible
and the other is not, the doctrines of the
one mentioned are bound to be the right
ones, or else why should the Church have
been mentioned at all ? Edicts having
come out against the Catholics (Charles of
blessed memory was very free and impartial

with his edicts), Archangel takes refuge in England—on the principle, perhaps, that the nearer the king the less likely was the edict to be put in force. On his way to England, luckily for him without the Spanish horse, he runs many dangers, once nearly falling into the clutches of his old friend the Calvinist preacher, who, in the train of the bishop he has fled to, is proceeding to London. Archangel hides in a wood, but his servant is taken, and in his baggage is found a chalice, which, according to the universal custom of Calvinists and Anglicans, the bishop and the ex-chaplain drink out of till at last they 'fall into the detestable vice of drunkenness.'

Arrived in London, his mother writes that all her property has been confiscated, so Archangel sends to the Guardian of the Capuchins (*el Guardian de los Capuchinos*) in Paris, to get the Queen of France to intercede with the English king, which she does, and the property is restored. He once more returns to Aberdeen ; but by this time, having doubtless become a well-known figure on the northern road, disguises himself as a hawker and visits his mother, whom he finds in a cottage, not knowing that her property has been restored. The neighbours, finding it impossible to stand more of Archangel's preaching, seize on him and send him by ship to England. On the voyage he reflects on the condition of Scotland, given over to the terrible plague of Calvinism—a plague, though, which seems to have endured long after Archangel's time.

From London he is removed to Rome, and on arriving there finds that Italy too is suffering from a terrible plague, but of a less persistent nature perhaps than the one affecting Scotland, being merely an outbreak of typhus fever. This happens in the year 1630, the solitary date, except that of Archangel's death, in the whole book. After his services in this plague honours descend upon Archangel, and he is made Guardian of the Convent of Monte Gorgio in the diocese of Fermo, and, according to the Padre Axofrin, close to the river of Lethe.

Some loadstone or other, though, always

seems to draw him to Scotland, for after a
year's residence at Monte Gorgio he starts
once more for that benighted land, this
time at the head of a Catholic mission.
At Cales (Calais) he meets the rest of the
mission, and takes ship with them in a
vessel of which the captain happens to
be a Catholic. In spite of the captain's
Catholicism a storm arises, as in fact it
always seems to have done when Archangel
put out to sea. Though 'disguised as a
gentleman' (and therefore perhaps as easily
recognisable through his disguise as many
who assume that character in more modern
times) the passengers discover he is a friar,
and, in order to appease the Moloch they
apparently adored, wished to throw him in
the sea to calm the tempest, thinking, it
seems, that Catholic friars are specially
obnoxious to the elements and to Moloch.
The Catholic captain speaks to the passengers, and offers to be thrown overboard
instead of Archangel. From this we
may judge that the *odium theologicum* had
not made so much way at sea as on shore,
for I believe the offer must have been

dictated by the sailor and not the Catholic
in the captain, and that a Protestant or
Mahommedan captain would probably have
done the same. This offer being refused,
and the crew and passengers being occupied,
as is customary in such cases, in casting lots
for the privilege of not being thrown overboard, the vessel strikes on a rock, and,
breaking into two halves, the after part
with the captain and crew is lost, and
Archangel and some of the mission and
passengers are cast on shore. A shepherd
informs the forlorn band that they have
been thrown on the ' Isle of Wicht,' and
that the well-known city of San Calpino
is near at hand. Well as I am used
to English names written phonetically in
Spanish, and recognising in an instant, as
I do, Whitehall masquerading as ' Quit-
vall,' Frobisher as ' Ofrisba,' Drake as
' El Draque,' and Westminster as ' Quest-
monster,' I confess that I can neither
recognise nor identify this San Calpino.
However, at this unknown town they in
due course arrive, and Archangel, for
reasons known to himself but not divulged

to a perhaps too curious public, takes the name of Selviano, after his mother's family name of Selvia, which, I confess, leaves me in the same position of agnosticism as does Sal Calpino.

Whilst taking their ease in the San Calpino inn they hear the King is at ' Neopurt,' not far off, and Archangel meets a young Scotch gentleman, who I saw at once must be his brother Edward. Such proves to be the fact, in spite of Archangel's own obtuseness, which delayed the recognition for some hours. They are mutually astonished at meeting one another in the Isle of White, so far removed from either Italy or Aberdeen, and in a place, as Edward well says, and as I myself have often reflected in that island, which is on the road to nowhere. Here Archangel hears of his mother's death, and the restitution of the family property.

Arrived at ' Neopurt,' they leave their cloaks and swords in the inn, and go out to view the fortification. It appears at that epoch that in Newport there was a celebrated tower said to be impregnable.

Edward, who, like most Scotchmen, had seen far better towers at home, began to scoff at it and to point out how easily with a few gentlemen of Aberdeen he could carry it at point of pike, and whilst discoursing of mamelons and ravelines and of the 'leaguer of Strigonium' is overheard and arrested for a spy. As the author well observes, 'the greatest injustices are always executed with the greatest exactitude' (he might have added also with the greatest promptitude), and Archangel and his brother are taken before the governor, and by him cast into prison. The King, hearing of their arrest, sends for them to interrogate them himself—though I confess I do not recognise the methods of Charles of blessed memory in this proceeding. With great show of probability, when we remember that we have been told that an edict had been specially promulgated against the Catholics, and that Archangel was named in it—or perhaps, indeed, it was to show how little he cared, through his divine right, for his own edict—Charles, on recognising Arch-

angel, whom he had known when interpreter to the Spanish Embassy, immediately
liberates him and his brother. Of the
rest of the passengers (and perhaps quite
properly) we hear no more, and of this I
care but little, except about the fate of the
Catholic captain, and on this point, alas!
the author is inexorable.

After some days at the court of 'Neopurt' Archangel starts again for Aberdeen,
sailing from the well-known port of Viklen,
which is still waiting for its Columbus as
far as I am concerned, for neither Cabot,
Ponce de Leon, Juan de la Cosa, or any of
those Spanish navigators who showed us
the world, seem to have visited it.

Here I may remark that, after a careful
perusal of his life, I have come to the con-
clusion that there was no port of Europe
in which, if Archangel found himself
stranded, he did not instantly find a ship
just sailing for Aberdeen; hence, I imagine,
the trade of Aberdeen was vastly more
considerable in the days of Charles the
First than it is at present, as, indeed, seems
not unlikely.

Arrived once more in Monomusco's halls, he throws himself into mission work with as much alacrity as if it had been the heart of Africa, and the place becoming once more too hot for him, he retreats to Edinburgh, the capital of Scotland, remarkable for having been the birthplace of Alexandro de Ales.

In Edinburgh one Baron Daltay (el Baron de Daltay), for whose name I have unsuccessfully searched in Nisbet's Heraldry, lies sick to death, and, being a Protestant, not unnaturally wishes to confess to a Catholic priest before his end. His friend Baron Balguay (whom Douglas's Peerage is powerless to assist me in identifying) brings in Archangel.

The Protestants, who seem to have been always on the alert for cases such as these (which happened frequently), rush into the house to kill Archangel, who only saves his life by jumping from a window. Balked of their victim, they fall (like theologians) on poor Baron Balguay and purge him of his heresy with their skeenes.

The author says a skeene (*esquin*) is

like an Albacete knife, and indeed it may
be, for one is straight and one is crooked.
Then, to free the land from Catholics, they
kill the son, aged ten, who, as the father
was a Protestant, most likely was one too ;
but when did ever theologians, when killing
was to be done, haggle at trifles of that
nature ?

Having seen enough of Edinburgh and
of the way they argued religious differences
there, Archangel, disguised as a physician,
goes to the province of Esterling, and there
at once sets to convert the sound and heal
the sick.

Throughout the book these little in-
dications show that Archangel was a
simple-minded honest fellow, doing what
he thought his duty at all hazards. This,
to my mind, appears so novel that I do not
doubt it happened three hundred years ago.
Though Padre Ajofrin never quotes a single
word Archangel says, I fancy I can see him
just as plainly as if, in the modern fashion,
he had spoken pages and never done a thing
worth doing.

The cures he effected were quite

wonderful, the author says, and then somewhat enigmatically observes he is unaware
if Archangel had ever studied medicine.
The fact he cured at all induces me to
believe that perhaps he had but little
previous knowledge. But be that as it
may, the doctors of Esterling (all trades-
unionists) look on his practising with great
disfavour. Whether they thought him
wanting in a knowledge of pathology, or
that a Catholic had no right to doctor
Protestants, does not appear, but anyhow
they forced him to leave Esterling and re-
tire to Aberdon. Hardly arrived there, a
royal messenger summons him to London,
but whether to answer for his tampering
with the faith of Aberdon, or to ascertain
whether he held a foreign medical degree,
remains uncertain. Archangel, ever ready
for a journey, starts at once, and at
Torfechan, on the borders of the kingdom
we are told, stays at an inn, in which he
meets a nobleman, Baron de Cluni, an
Englishman (*sic*), whom he converts, with
all his retinue. Just about to start for
London, he is taken ill with a fever, gets

worse, and ends his journey and the journey of his life in 1637.

By night the Catholics of the retinue of the Baron, with a priest who happened to be in the neighbourhood disguised, carry the body, dressed in the Capuchin habit, and bury it in a wild and desert place in the hills, far from the dwellings of mankind. They mark the grave with a simple slab of slate, and water it with blood disguised in tears (*sangre disimulada en lagrimas*).

Thus ends, says Padre Ajofrin, the life of him who in the world was called George Leslie (Jorge Lesleo), born to much honours, wealth, and titles, and in religion known as Father Archangel, and who passed his life in poverty, in journeyings, and in good works. From it we may learn, remarks the author, obedience, truthfulness, humility, and holy caution, and how ingenious is charity in God's saints. They may be so, though for 'ingenious charity' somehow one seems not to be much 'enthused.'

What I discern is that Archangel was a

simple-minded friar who did his duty as he thought he saw it, and did it for itself and not for honour or reward or hope of heaven, nor yet for fear of hell. I care but little that ' this servant of the Lord ' published a book divided in two parts and titled ' De Potestate Pontificis Romani,' and which the learned and ingenious Wadingo cites, or if he had written nothing ; I like him for his life of sturdy failure.

Possibly in England and in Scotland, far from the dwellings of mankind, on hill and moor, there sleep under rough slates many who like Archangel struggled manfully to stop the march of time and bring back yesterday. Well, peace be with them. To me those lonely burial-places now forgotten, so silent, buried in mist and lost on hill, fit graves for those who fail, mean more than all the pomps of alabaster with due mendacious epitaph in church or synagogue.

Now that Aberdeenshire is free from his assaults, and could we find it in Torfechan, over his deserted grave, even the Calvinist, I take it, would not refrain from saying with Padre Ajofrin, when thinking of the simple - minded Capuchin, ' Pretiosa in conspectu Domini est mors sanctorum ejus.'

R. B. C. G.

II

A WILL

BEFORE me is a thin quarto volume bound
in vellum, stained and yellow by the ages
during which it has lain unmolested in the
archives of Avila.   It is tied together with
strings of parchment.   On loosing them
one finds a manuscript written in characters
strange, twisted, picturesque, enigmatical
to all but those who have made a long
study of deciphering old handwritings.   It
is a will, and unlike modern wills, gives us
some clue to the character, throws across the
centuries some shadow of the living figure
of whose last wishes it is the guardian.   A
will, every clause of which is a duty per-
formed, an act of charity or of justice,
every disposition of which was thought
out carefully and slowly, as if the conveying

43

of each individual item to paper was to be an everlasting burden or a relief to the conscience of the testator in the inevitable blank beyond the tomb. A will that cost long hours of prayer before the shrines of many churches, much unwearying consultation with confessors, Jesuits, and others, much pondering over the construction of every phrase before the 'notary public.' Master Gaspar or Blas, or whatever his name was who gave it its definitive form, stamped on it his notarial seal and rubrica,[1] in testimony of its truth and his own fidelity.

And as one reads it, it seems as if a window opened into the past and the figure of the old Castilian gentleman who loved, fought, suffered, and struggled, over three centuries ago, shapes itself firmly out of the shadowy dimness and takes definite form and outline.

The precise date of his birth is unknown. The date of his death is undecipherable on the grey slab under which he lies in the

---

[1] Rubrica, *i.e.* rubric, is the flourish at the end of a signature. Without the rubrica the signature was not valid in law. Hence the saying, ' Mas reale rubrica que firma.'

Discalced Carmelite Church of Avila, 'which,' he says in this same will, not without some pride and intimate satisfaction, ' I myself built at my own expense.'

The details of his life are few and vague. He was a gentleman of means. His possessions lay scattered in the hills and plains of Avila.

In the little rugged village of Colillas, that looks about a handbreadth off in the clear searching air and is three leagues ; in Serranillos, the rough mountain hamlet at the head of the pass between Avila and Estremadura ; at Muñosancho, at Xemerandura, and in other places now difficult to identify he owned yugadas[1] of land, *pan de trigo y pan terciado*, producing wheat and other crops in succession. Besides his scattered territorial possessions, his cornfields, flax-fields, and villages, his woods and pasture-grounds, he owned in spite of piety many a productive mortgage over the entailed estates of others.

Many a time before religion weaned him

---

[1] A yugada was as much as an ox could plough. In Scotland it was called an ' oxgangis.'

from material interests, he rode out of
Avila, a black figure, his long cloak sweeping down over the horse's quarters, by the
first light of day to visit them ; many
nights the stars twinkling over the battlements of the city welcomed him on his
return. That he was a hard master to his
labourers is impossible. That he was exact
to the last farthing in his accounts with
them is certain. But it was the exactitude
that is followed by generosity. All these
possessions small and great, calculated to
the last yugada of ground, to the last fanega[1]
of grain, are scheduled in his will. But
then he was only the steward, and had to
render an accurate reckoning. Had it not
been so, what of his nieces, nuns in the
Convent of Sta. Maria, to whom he leaves
12 ducats a piece, besides paying down
their dower to the convent? What of the
Benedictine Monastery, to which certain
possessions of his wife's had belonged, and
which must now return to Holy Mother
Church, unshorn of a tittle of their value?
Kindly, formal, courteous, sweet of nature,

---

[1] A fanega is about a hundredweight.

and holy of life we know he was from contemporaneous testimony—so holy that he was known in Avila as the Holy Gentleman. His wife was Da. Mencia del Aguila, one of the noblest amongst the many noble families of Avila. She brought him possessions as extensive as his own. He and his wife as long as she lived worked hand in hand, and lightened the lives of many poor neighbours,—he too lightened various souls of their heavy burdens by his judicious counsels and soothing consolations. He was a familiar figure in all the convent locutories, and was beloved alike of saintly mother-prioresses and father-abbots. His household was tranquil, full of Christian kindliness and good-will : so says his nephew, who lived with him,—one amongst the many recipients of his large-hearted bounty, —in a book which has long ceased to exist.

At the head of it was a certain old housekeeper, a type which has disappeared with the simple patriarchal age it belonged to, the devoted friend rather than a servant in the house she ruled. A woman that her master and mistress treated with respect, and loved not as a dependent but as one belonging to them, whom even they never addressed without her title Sra. Ospedal, a woman so upright and Godfearing that when her master shall be lying dead in the bed he describes so minutely, she shall not be required to swear to, or give any account of the jewels, the silver, and other valuables under her charge, ' for,' says he, ' she is so good a Christian and of so fine a conscience, that whatever she will say will be the truth.'

On his wife's death he became a Jesuit and a priest. How long he laboured in the company of Jesus we do not know. The one date we can be certain of is the date of the will, signed on the 7th of April, the year of the birth of Jesus Christ 1579.

It begins not with possessions but with the soul. This writing of a will is a solemn moment to a Spaniard. It was with the black shadow of Death already shrouding his thoughts that he dictated the opening paragraph (for no notary could have evolved a note of such sincerity, earnestness, and belief).

' jesus In Dei nomine, let it be to all who shall see this testamentary letter and last will a manifest and notorious thing, how I, Francisco de Salcedo, priest and native of this very noble city of Avila, minding me of death that it is a natural and certain thing, and the hour of it most uncertain, and considering how convenient a thing it is that I should settle what is necessary for my salvation in time, and dispone of the goods which our Lord has given me by His infinite mercy for His holy service ; for this cause, believing as I believe in the most Holy Trinity, Father, Son, and Holy Spirit, three persons, and one only true God, and all the rest that Holy Mother Church holds, believes, and confesses, in which faith I protest I live and die as a Catholic and Christian, being, as I am, sound in body and in my right mind and natural understanding, I grant, and re-cognise by this present letter I am making, and order this my testament and last will to the service of God our Lord and His blessed mother in the following manner :—

' First, I commend my soul to God, our

Lord Jesus Christ, who made and redeemed it with His precious blood, and my body to the earth of which it was made, and I order that when our Lord is pleased to take me from this present life my body be buried in the Church of Señor San Pablo, which is adjoining the Church of Señor San Josef of this city, which I made and built at my expense, from its beginning.'

As to the funeral, the honours, the mass, the wax, and the offering, these he remits to his legatees. But it pleases the old man, as he follows in spirit his own imaginary funeral procession through the silent streets of his native city, amidst the deep tolling of the cathedral bell and the bells of many monasteries and convents, to know that in the little Church of San Pablo the friends of his life—the good Master Daza, Gonzalo de Aranda, and Julian de Avila—shall say and sing their masses over the upturned face of him who was once their comrade. Nevertheless, so that all may be done seemly, fifty-two masses are to be said as speedily as possible for the repose of his soul in San Pablo, fifty masses each in the monastery churches of Sto. Tomás and San Francisco, and yet another fifty in the College of San Millán.

In the cathedral of Avila, nailed on one of the pillars, close to the west gateway, a little blue Talavera plaque still beseeches of the faithful alms for the wretched captives languishing in the Baths of Tunis or Tripoli. The need for it has gone, although the plaque remains. That blue and white plaque, to-day merely a relic of times gone by, was for Francisco de Salcedo a daily reminder of an obligation, and he leaves to the redemption of captives *lo acostumbrado*, the sum he had ever been accustomed to give. If he remembers forgotten captives in Tunis, his servitors in Avila are not forgotten. His clothes and shirts are to be distributed amongst them, and Sra. Ospedal is to dole them out as she thinks fit. Two ducats are to be given to the sons of Agustin, the son of Maria Diaz, ' for what I may owe him, if I owe him anything, and even if I do not.'

He sets apart a portion of his house, viz. the apartment presently occupied by the Sr.

Pablo Xuarez, consisting of a room with its
alcobas and two sleeping places over the
corral, and a little cellar underneath opening
into the zaguan for Mistress Ospedal, 'free
of rent or any other thing, and no one shall
be able to cast her out.' It is pathetic to
see how tenderly solicitous he is about the
little comforts of his old housekeeper. She
is to open if she likes a door from the room
to the zaguan,[1] but nevertheless she is still
free to use the patio as before. There she
is to live with her servants for all the days
of her life, and over and above is to take
such jewels and furniture, to be chosen and
pointed out by herself, as amount to the
value of 12 ducats. Nor shall Mistress
Ospedal be bullied and worried by scriveners
or legatees. 'Neither the heir nor any
other person shall require of her any account
whatever, either of bread, or money, or
silver, or valuables, or furniture, or anything else that she may have had or has
under her charge until the day of my death ;
and when that shall take place she is to be

---

[1] Zaguan is the porch between the door and the patio (court).
It is an Arabic word, which means 'covered.'

believed on her word alone, and the usual
oath is to be done away with, because I hold
her for so good a Christian that one can
trust her and her conscience, and I am
certain she will keep nothing belonging to
me or any one else.

'Ana, my servant, daughter of Maria
Ceveca, besides 10 ducats, is to have the
bed I sleep on, with its two mattresses, a
blanket, and a coloured counterpane, and
two sheets, two pillows, and another bed
made of rope (*cordeles*).'

There is an old house in Avila, close to
the Archbishop's Palace, in Salcedo's time
the Jesuit College of San Gil. Both house
and palace form part of the famous walls of
Avila, which shows that they were in other
times the fortified dwellings of the old
conquistadores who wrested the city from
the Moors, and whose proud duty it was to
guard the ramparts. A half-defaced coat-
of-arms hangs over the doorway which leads
into the patio—the famous patio into
which Sra. Ospedal was to have, in Scotch
legal phraseology, 'free ish and entrance.'
The patio is dank, grown over with straggling

grass and trees. In the centre there is the well. A few indigent families now inhabit the dwelling of the old Castilian hidalgo, although, from the proverbial incuria of the Spanish character, it still retains traces of its ancient and more honourable uses. The last of the Salcedos, a little official in Madrid still draws its rents, but between him and his ancestor there is a great gulf fixed. As to its interior, it is only a convent that can give any adequate idea of its stateliness, its grave repose, and the dignity of the surroundings.

The brief clause in which he bequeaths his most valued belongings to the Church of San José shows what was its furniture. To it he bequeaths all his Flemish tapestries (*lienços de Flandes*) and images that he may leave ; ' also all that is in the oratory that I have in my house, with its Spanish leather (*guardamecíes*), altar, and chests, and looking-glass, and all the rest I have, and which may be found within my said oratory on the day of my death ; and moreover all the ornaments (*hornamento*), chalices, and chest in which is contained all the other things I have for saying and serving mass ;

and moreover three carpets that I have, so that all that may be the property of the said Church of San Pablo, and for its use and adornment ; and moreover I bequeath it two French chairs (*sillas francesas*), so that they may remain in the said church for ever.'

Indeed a church was the only fitting place for such treasures to repose in, for the stately beauty of them may be dimly imagined in the dry enumeration signed by the notary public. There, where was his grave, it was most fitting that on great and solemn festivals, the Flemish tapestries should hang from the aisles, their gigantic figures lit up by the flickering flame of torches and wax tapers. It consoled him to know that the ornaments which had served him so long would have a still nobler use than in the oratory of a private house; that the *sillas francesas* would eternally abide, one on each side of the high altar, and that the Bishops of Avila, succeeding each other like shadows, would one and all make use of the gifts of his bounty.

I am glad to say that, perishable as are dead men's last wishes and comminations, that the chairs still stand in the place allotted to them by the donor who died three centuries ago, and to-day is forgotten as he had never been in the Avila into which he had intertwined his life.

Indeed this same Discalced Convent of Avila, founded by one Teresa of Jesus, whom he had loved and comforted ever since, an introspective and wretched young nun in the Encarnacion, she had confided to him the agonies of her soul, was the object of the old man's dearest predilections. For the endowment 'dote,' building and repairs, lamp, and ornament of the Church of San Pablo, and for the maintenance of a sacristan to take care of the ornaments and things belonging to it, to keep it clean and swept and in good order, and to assist at the masses which shall be said in it, he leaves all his hereditaments and lands situated in Xemerandura, close to Hontiberos, with its houses and all belonging to it, consisting of over two yugadas of land, which produce 166 fanegas of grain, half wheat and half oats, so that they become the property of San Pablo for ever. From this fund is also to be provided the wax, wine, and consecrated wafers free of charge to all the priests who there said mass, and 1000 maravedises of annual salary to a priest who personally, and without committing the charge to any other person, shall bind himself to say, and shall say every week of the year, four masses in the Church of San Pablo for the souls of such as he may choose. Of the soul of the founder (himself) Salcedo, with a refinement of self-denial and a feeling closely approaching to heroism, makes no stipulation. In a parenthesis he adds softly and apologetically, like the humble and unworthy Christian he felt himself to be, 'I ask him of his charity to pray to God for me,' and without any trace of emphasis adds simply that his appointment is to be made in accordance with a paper which 'I and the nuns of San José have drawn up between us.'

Nor were these the only gifts to his

favourite convent. To it he left his lands
of La Nava, with all its woods, pasturages,
and houses ; to it he left his hamlets of
La Colilla and Cortos. Not only so, but
in an unhappy moment for the nuns and
his heirs,—for his act involved a lawsuit
which cost the contending parties more
than the property was worth, and was only
ended in 1849, when the government appro-
priated the whole of the territorial possessions owned by the religious bodies of
Spain, — he wrested for their benefit the
lands of Muñosancho from the entail under
which he had succeeded to them.

But if the nuns receive benefits so great,
they contract a debt no less great and
onerous,—a debt which they are bound to
pay so long as they and the convent remain
in existence. For all time coming on the
anniversary of his interment, or if it falls
on some solemn festival within the octave
of the same, they bind themselves and the
generations after them to sing a mass for
souls in purgatory.

'And I desire,' adds Salcedo solemnly,
'that this may not be postponed to any

future obligation, but I charge it on their consciences that they keep and fulfil it in respect of the said estates which I leave them for that purpose, and as a charitable bequest.'

In Spanish convents an official register is kept, often dating back many centuries, in which every successive prioress enters the names of all who have given alms to or benefited the community. No matter whether it is the rich man's lands or the poor man's pence, there the names lie embedded side by side to all eternity. The community has contracted a solemn obligation to its benefactors, and to accomplish this is as much a part of the routine of their lives as the ordinary conventual discipline. It may be doubted, with so many donations to convents and monasteries, whether Salcedo had any heir.

But the man who remembers first of all his soul, and then his faith, and then his charity, does not forget his duty to posterity.

To Marcos de Salcedo, his nephew, youngest son of the licentiate Adrada, he leaves 30 fanegas of land *de pan de renta* in

the confines of Picamixo for all the days
of his life, after which it is to revert to the
entail. To him also he leaves a mortgage
of 30,000 maravedises over the property of
Don Diego Mexia, which said mortgage
also belongs to the entailed estate, and
after his death shall revert to it again.

For a religious man like Salcedo, and at
a time when the canonical law so strongly
deprecated as sinful the possession of
mortgages, he seems to have held a considerable number of them. For in the
next breath he leaves to his nephew a
second perpetual mortgage of 1050 maravedises, which is also entailed on his heirs.
Perhaps, like the regular Castilian he was,
he was of opinion that *todos los males con
pan son menos*. To him also he leaves
the old fortified house, which he describes
as 'the principal houses where I dwell.'

There is a very curious clause relating
to Marcos de Salcedo, which illustrates the
spirit of the age in a very graphic manner.
Item—'I will that the whole of the said
houses and the rest of the estates which in
this my testament I bequeath to Marcos

de Salcedo, the younger, which belong to
the said entail, he shall enjoy and possess
for his life only, and afterwards after his
death, or if before it, he shall put *himself
into religion* (become a monk) ; then Da.
Maria de Salcedo, daughter of Agustin
de la Serna, shall have and inherit them
all, for herself and her heirs and successors.'
Marcos de Salcedo *did* become a monk, and
Agustin de la Serna succeeded to the entail.

This same entail had cost old Salcedo
many uneasy hours in life, for it was the
cause of a lawsuit between him and his
nephew, the said Agustin de la Serna. It
had been the cause of long whisperings in
the confessional, of much consultation with
learned Jesuits and others versed in canonical
law, such as the Dr. Rueda, who was also
in the most critical hours of her life the
adviser of Sta. Teresa. Fancy a man now
seeking legal advice from a Jesuit and a
cathedral canon instead of that domestic
tyrant, his family solicitor !

This lawsuit he transferred by his will
to the nuns of San José, who, from his death
until 1849 (when the convents were relieved

by a careful and economical State of all their territorial possessions), were ever waging war, wordy and otherwise, with the despiteful and litigious heirs of entail. Let the old man die content, however, and peaceful, dreaming neither of past lawsuits nor future ones, satisfied that his last wishes shall be respected, and happy in the prospect of his own tranquil rest under the grey slab of San Pablo.

Imagination—that feeble picture-maker—may see the last impressive scene, may even strive to render it to others, and be partially successful. Still we are dealing with realities. There, in that quiet little plaza, shrouded to-day in green, are the doors of the house, now worm-eaten and shaking on their hinges, whence he passed out for the last time, surrounded by his fellow-townsmen, to his eternal resting-place within the walls of San José. The silent streets of the grey old town through which, escorted by all the stately and old-fashioned pomp of torch and candle, the dead Francisco de Salcedo was borne on that funeral day, to which he refers solemnly as 'the day of my burial,' although the life of the sixteenth century which then floated through them has left to us only the rumour of its passage, are but little changed.

Watch a funeral to-day in Avila. See the many-robed confraternities as they fall into procession around the bier, and the priests in their violet robes going before, chanting solemn and lugubrious responses. Listen to the bells tolling from the cathedral, echoing through space and arousing that sentiment which dwells in all of us—of the irrevocable and the past, and the quick passage of Humanity into Oblivion. As the dull thud of them strikes the ear, as earth upon the coffin, their sound is taken up by the tinkling response from monastery and convent tower.

The white coifed, mysterious figures who, hidden in the shadowy depths behind the grating bars, watch the old man's corpse as it lies in state for the space of one night and one day before the altar of their convent church, are the same now as then. Centuries have passed, but these strange communities conserve and revere all the footprints of the generations who trod the cloister floors before them.

Through the dusky aisles of San Millán, San Francisco, and San Gil those fifty masses each shall be sung with all due and mournful solicitude. San Francisco lies a heap of ruins at the outskirts of the town ; San Millán has become a seminary, the Jesuit College of San Gil, the Bishops' Palace. Time has waved his transforming wand, and they are now mere memories. Still, there it all is, and it only wants a little touch to lift the veil, and amidst much that has changed, more that is Dead, and past memories still living, it only needs this old yellow will, three centuries old, for us to see a figure, very firmly and finely shaped, of the bounteous master and chivalrous gentleman who left Sra. Ospedal to mourn for him alone in the desolation of her old age, and once paced through Avila, solemn, stately, and kindly, as if he and his age were to be remembered there for ever. G. C. G.

III

DE HERETICO COMBURENDO

VALLADOLID, from Belad el Walid—that is, in Arabic, the Land of Walid, once the capital of Spain, and now a dull, decaying town in Old Castille, on the Pisuerga.

Few places even in Spain recall more forcibly the past. On every side a plain stretching for miles, to the north the mountains dimly visible, on the south and east and west plains, and more plains.

No commerce, little traffic, few modern buildings except a court for the *pelota* (the national game of ball), to which the inhabitants draw your attention with pride as evidence of coming prosperity. Even the bull ring seems decaying. No bicycles, but few advertisements, and these chiefly of things that no one can have any use for.

Still, an air of ancient splendour hangs about the town. In the arcaded plazas many a heretic has purged his contempt by fire, and gone, perhaps to heaven, perhaps from fire to fire. In every street a ruined palace, at every turn a house in which lived some one known in history ; an air that only having been a capital ever imparts. In the Plazuela del Ochavo, where the Emperor Charles V. pardoned the Comuneros, still stands the house, with the window bars not yet repaired, where Philip II. was baptized. The bars were cut to show the infant to the people.

Just the sort of town in which one might expect to find a Scottish and an English Catholic College. Philip, of pious memory (in Spain), founded them both. Perhaps his motives were political, perhaps religious. Who in England can judge of motives in Spain? As easily as a Spaniard can judge of morals in England. Climate, I take it, influences both, as it does judgments. Mary, in England 'bloody,' in Spain is 'pious.' Claver-house, a fiend in Ayrshire, is a hero in the Highlands. Still we owe Philip gratitude for his two colleges, if only to remind us that we too were persecutors.

In a long rambling street the Scottish College stands. The natives (of the poorer sort) speak of the College as *el colegio de los Escorozeces*, giving the word an extra syllable, perhaps for euphony. Still they add they are good Christians, and this is the highest praise men of their kind in Spain can give.

Hard by the College Cervantes lived and wrote the second part of *Don Quixote*; close by Columbus died poor and broken-hearted; not far off dwelt Gondomar. A bit of Scotland lost in Castille, and yet a place no Scotsman (even a Presbyterian) should behold unmoved.

Many in Scotland are the tales of suffering and persecution that Protestants endured, but never does one hear of the tyranny that forced a Scottish Catholic to seek his education at Douay, Valladolid, and St. Omer. How many Scotsmen have heard of the Scoto-Spanish College? How many have visited it? Yet thoroughly to

comprehend the faith sufficient to move
mountains and extirpate humanity in man,
which reigned in Scotland in times past,
it must be visited. Much has the Odium
Theologicum to answer for in Scotland and
other lands. How admirable, when thinking of it, appears the simple faith of the
savages of whom some traveller relates that
of whatever faith the missionary was, into
the hot stone oven straight he went.

Passing the ponderous door, set in a
horse-shoe arch, the present melts away.
On every side the past looks down on one.
A flagged and vaulted corridor leads to a
long refectory, with the table set, as in the
' Cena ' of Leonardo, with bread, and jugs
of rough Valencian pottery. Mary Queen
of Scots looks through the gloaming
from the wall ; Semple of Semple (a pious
founder) faces her. Out of every corner
Scottish Jesuits of the past seem to appear.
Across the passage seem to emerge the
shades of Scottish priests, who in their
lifetime had lurked in Scottish castle and
Elizabethan manor-house, and occupied
the secret chamber in the houses of the

English and Scottish Catholics. At once
the air of rest and quiet seems to suggest
the College as a fitting place in which to
rear up men to minister to scattered Catholic
communities in Aberdeenshire, Lochaber,
and Strathglass.

Scholars—some twenty, chiefly peasants'
sons from Aberdeenshire ; priests — three
or four ; lastly, the Rector. Only in
Redgauntlet and in books of Jacobites does
such a priest exist. I fancy the Rector of
the Scottish Castilian College is the last
surviving type. Scotissimus Scotorum,
a Scot of Scots, tall, thin, and sinewy, a
Highlander, a scholar and linguist, withal
a gentleman, with the geniality that
Presbyterianism seems to have crushed out
of the modern Scotsman. In talking with
him one seems to see what sort of men
the Scotsmen of the past had been before
the worship of the Bawbee and the Bible
had altered them. Something quite unlike
Scotland in the urbanity of the man ; a
sort of being, as it were, in community with
the rest of Europe, instead of, as at present,
condemned to fellowship with only Germans

(High and Low), Dutchmen, and Scandinavians; people who, excellent no doubt, have nothing of the Slave or Latin interest about them. Just the kind of man who in old days was charged with missions by the Pope, 'the King of Spain,' or Mary Queen of Scots, to save the somewhat scabby, if faithful sheep who still remained in Scotland. If the world had only gone on right (or wrong) Father M'Donald had been enthroned at Edinburgh, at Brechin, or St. Andrews, 'a fayre prelate,' with cope and chasuble, crosier and ring of amethyst on his forefinger, with candle, bell and book, and power to curse the heretic and lift the finger in the attitude, so dear to bishops, of malediction. As it is, a Scoto-Spanish priest and gentleman speaking Castilian faintly tinged with Gaelic, and dinning education and religion into fledgling Scoto-Spanish or Hispano-Scottish priests.

Nature or fate is, very prodigal of men, not in the way of turning out many, fitted to excel in anything but cheapening bicycles, but in another fashion. When in a million a man is born fitted to rule the Church, lead men, or to direct a country, ten to one that fate or nature sets him to do that which the million others could have done as well as he, and leaves his task to fools.

Over the Scottish College hangs an air of Scotland, but not of Scotland of to-day, but of that older Scotland that was poor and furnished soldiers and adventurers to all the rest of Europe ; that Scotland which vanished after Culloden, and has been replaced by factories and mines, progress and money, and an air of commonplace, exceeding all the world.

Not looking over carefully at the writing of St. Thomas of Aquinas, the autograph of Her of Avila, the relics (all authentic), the rich groined roof so finely arched, or even at the curious wooden flooring of the church, unique in Spain, I say farewell to my compatriots and out into the street, thanking my stars for the chance of having seen that which enabled me to reconstruct the Scotland of the past more vividly than by perusing libraries.

In the Calle Real de Don Sancho, as

close to the Scottish College as Gretna is to Carlisle, stands the Colegio de los Ingleses. Founded, like the other, by Philip II., the English College was designed to commemorate the triumph of the Invincible Armada. The 'Invincible' is long dispersed ; its sailors from Biscay and from Catalonia have left their bones on Achill and upon the Hebrides ; all of it has disappeared with the exception of here and there a rusty anchor, but here and there a darker cheek in Galway or a brighter eye amongst the ponies of the coast. Had it succeeded, without doubt to-day we had all been Catholics, and the poor Catholic gentleman of Garstang, mentioned by Froude, had been relieved from the obligation of going on Sunday to 'take wine' with the vicar at the parish church. The College still remains, apparently unchanged since its foundation.

The work begun by Campion, Parsons, and their fellows, still goes on. The corridors through which they paced, reading their breviaries, remain identical. The pupils (more ruly, let us fain hope, than their predecessors, of whom the Jesuit fathers had to complain at Rome) still sit down in the self-same stone refectory.

In England how few remember the disgraceful page of history that the fantastic tortures and the martyrdoms of the Jesuits in the pictures hanging on the wall attest. Let them rest on, secure at least in one thing, that the torments that a hard world inflicts on their descendants defy the limner's power to put in pictures, even with a knowledge of perspective.

If the Scots College had an air of Scotland, so the English College has an air of prosperous England ; but how unlike the other. The self-same architecture, the self-same iron-studded doors, the altars in the style of Churriguera in the chapels, where saints and angels float in a sea of gilded gingerbread, identical, but still an outward air and inward grace making them different, as Thurso is from Yeovil.

Why is it that the races English and Scotch have never really amalgamated ? So close, so like, both wizened by the same east wind, tormented more or less by the same Sunday, and yet unlike, and so the colleges. St. George for Merrie England. No one in his wildest fits of patriotism ever talked of Merrie Scotland. Did Knox kill merriment, even as Macbeth did murder sleep? Loyal, abstemious, business-like, haggis-eating, tender, disagreeable, true, a Scotsman may be, but merry never.

An air of Oxford pervades the English College, all seems so prosperous, so old-established, and so English. The well-stocked library, with its rows of fine old Spanish, Latin, and English books clothed in white vellum, lettered on the backs in strange old-fashioned hands; the comfortable reading-desks and well-warmed room, all spoke of England. Not that there were not things unusual to be seen in English colleges. The pictures on the wall of English Catholics, martyred for conscience' sake by so-called freedom-loving Englishmen, gave a different note. These are particulars it pleases me to dwell on. Pleasant to slap one's chest and say, 'I am an Englishman;' to think that in my country every faith is free, from Christianity to Obi worship, free and untrammelled as long as it observes the laws of decency and of the Stock Exchange. It pleases me to think that if the cruel Duke of Alva racked and burnt and scourged the Protestants of Holland, Elizabeth of England was not a jot inferior to him in her dealings with English Catholics. Is it to be allowed that Catholics shall have the copyright of persecution ? Perish the thought ; Christians of all denominations have shown their love to one another by the rack and stake. Certain it is Pizarro and Cortes depopulated empires, but they at least imagined that their mission in the Indies (after the gold was found) was to convert the Indians. Besides, the Spanish butcheries ceased with the sixteenth century. Ours have continued almost to the present day. Where are the natives of Tasmania, the Australian blacks, the greater portion of the Maories ? Is it to be believed that we exterminated these men out of a desire to save their souls ?

After the martyrs' pictures the chief glory of the place is the image of the Blessed Virgin richly carved in wood. Powerful in miracles (*muy milagrosa*) the people of the town affirm her, and why should any doubt it? During the sack of Cadiz the heathen soldiers (so runs the Spanish story) of the Count of Essex tore this Virgin from her shrine, and to display their Christian toleration hacked off her arm and drew it through the streets tied to a string. After the sack, and when the pagans had returned to England, what could an English College do better than show its faith by offering an asylum to the poor image maltreated by the English who in England denied the faith? So in procession they received her, with music, incense, and with acolytes, and placed her where she stands to-day, blackened with age, but comely and most miraculous.

Each name upon the lists on the refectory walls has had its tragedy. Tichbornes and Babingtons, Englefields and Catesbys, jostle one another. They set one thinking on the past, and on the way in which all history is written to suit the conscience of the conquerors. The world has always readily come out to greet the conqueror with trumpets and with flowers ; but he has always had to conquer first. The names upon the walls are names of beaten men, and speak of causes long forgotten. Neither racks nor calumny can further harm them, and in their time they had their fill of both. Therefore I take it that without incurring *scandalum magnatum* a man may drop his literary tear upon their memory. At any rate, if freedom has been won by martyrdom, to the Campions, Garners, and the rest we owe as much as to the men who perished at Smithfield or upon the moors of Galloway. And if they did not snuffle through the nose, or take the names of Hebrew worthies, instead of calling themselves plain George or John, they were as truly martyrs, and their state, for all I know, as gracious.

So out into the deserted sandy street, between its *tapia* walls, to muse upon the colleges, and to reflect that had not stake and rack and red-hot pincers proved so efficacious, perchance the England of to-day had been as Catholic as Belgium.

R. B. C. G.

IV

IN THE TARUMENSIAN WOODS

Strange that reason should so often go astray, but that digestion should be unerring. So it is, though. The greatest minds have fallen into error. There is no recorded instance of even a congenital idiot having deceived his digestion. It may be, then, that after all reason is not the highest attribute of humanity.

Be that as it may, reason, in its eternal conflict with faith, seldom comes off so badly as when it encounters prejudice. So inveterate is prejudice and so shamefaced is reason, that one sometimes wonders whether faith and prejudice are not synonymous.

Few prejudices are so inveterate, and therefore on few questions is so little reason displayed, as on the subject of the Jesuits.

To be a member of the Society of Jesus conveys to many excellent people the impression that a sort of baccalaureate of lying, of chicanery, and of casuistry has been attained. It would seem that a Jesuit is a man perpetually, for no particular object, endeavouring to deceive the world, and even himself. Macchiavelli is his favourite author, Suarez his dearest study, and his political ideal that of Ezzelino da Romano, or Malatesta of Rimini. In history, when a king was murdered or dethroned, a queen poisoned, a conspiracy hatched, or a revolution attempted, the blame was thrown upon the Jesuits, with or without proof, in the same impartial way as it is now thrown upon the Anarchists. In both cases no doubt the desired result was attained, and a scapegoat acquired on which to lay the sins of others. Humanity dearly loves a scapegoat.

Nothing in all the Mosaic Dispensation appears to me to show more clearly the profound knowledge of the human heart possessed by its compiler than the institution of the sin-bearing quadruped. If the people were worth the sacrifice of the goat appears doubtful after a perusal of their history, and it might have been prudent, one would have thought, to hesitate before sacrificing the unoffending animal.

The Jesuits were said to be self-seekers in the Indies and schemers in Europe.

True, St. Francis Xavier was a Jesuit; and few, after reading his life, would accuse him of being a schemer or a self-seeker, and, after reading his hymn, I should imagine that the doubts of any one would be removed. Still, perhaps he was the exception that proved the rule; though how exceptions prove rules has not been vouchsafed to us at present.

By a curious fatality, not only Catholics and Protestants, but also freethinkers, were united against them, and their only defenders were Rousseau, Raynal, Mably, and Montesquieu. Even Felix de Azara, impartial as he was on most matters, and amiable, as his celebrated dedication to his History of Paraguay clearly shows him to have been, became a violent partisan when writing of the Jesuits. That in Paraguay, at all events, the Jesuits were not all self-seekers and plotters, that they accomplished much good, endured great perils and hardships, and were the only people whose mere presence did not bring mortality amongst the Indians, I hope to try to prove at some length at the proper time and place. Meanwhile I have to deal with the adventures of one particular Jesuit, a kindly, honest, simple-minded man, whose lot was thrown in strange places, and who fortunately has preserved for us a record of his undertakings.

On the eve of St. John, but without chronicling the year, except more or less (*año de* 1756 *mas o menos*), did he, so to speak, strike the Gospel trail from San Joaquin in Paraguay, accompanied by some Guaraní neophytes ; but this demands a little explication.

In the last century the Jesuits had gathered most of the Guaraní Indians in Paraguay, and what has now become the Argentine province of Corrientes, into

some thirty little towns or missions, known
to the country people as *capillas* (chapels),
and extending from Guayrá, near the
cataract of the Paraná, to Yapeyú, on the
Uruguay. On this somewhat stony vine-
yard they worked unceasingly, instilling
not only theology, but some tincture of
civilisation, into the Guaranís.

The Tobás, the Guaycurús, the Mocobíos, then as now roamed the swampy
wilderness of the Gran Chaco, the Great
Hunting Ground (Chaco in Guarani signifies a hunting-ground) of the remnant of
the tribes who fled from Peru and Chile
on the advance of Almagro and Pizarro,
and from Bolivia and the Argentine Republic before Solís and the Mendozas,
to wander in its recesses. In the little
town of San Joaquin, called Tarumá by
the Jesuits, on account of the forests of
tarumá-trees which surrounded it, there
dwelt the chronicler of the following little
episode.

He was a member of the crafty, schem-
ing Society of Jesus, it should be remembered, so that no doubt his writings had

an esoteric meaning. From his youth he had been engaged in missionary work.

Like Moffat and like Livingstone, he burned with zeal to change the faith of men who had done him no previous injury, and, like them, having begun his labours, his humanity rose superior to his dogma. In those days no paragraphs in newspapers, no plaudits from a close-packed audience in Exeter Hall, at intervals of a year or two, no testimonials, no pious teas ; nothing but drudgery amongst savages, but journeys, ridings by night and day, sleeping amongst swamps, fightings and preachings, and death at last of fever, or by Indian club or arrow.

For all reward, calumny and misconception, and a notice in the appendix of a book written by a member of the Society, in this wise :—

Padre Julian Lizardi, a Biscayan, caught by the Chiriguanos, tied to a stake, and shot to death with arrows.

Diego Herrera, pierced with a spear.

Lucas Rodriguez, slain at the altar by the Mocobíos.

Gaspar Osorio, killed and eaten by the Payaguás.

84

In those days a missionary, even a
Jesuit, had to bear his cross ; not that the
missionary of to-day does not ascend his
little Calvary, but still I fancy that the
pebbles in the road are not so lumpy, and
that the road itself is better fit for bicycles.
Thrice had my Jesuit crossed the Pampas
from Buenos Ayres to Mendoza, as he tells
us. Often had he travelled amongst the
Tobás and the Abipones ; amongst the
Guaycurús, 'most turbulent of heathen, who
extract their eyelashes to better see the
Christians, and to slay them ; their bodies
painted many colours ; worshipping no
gods, except, perhaps, their horses, with
whom they are more truly of one flesh
than with their wives.' In perils oftentimes
amongst the Payaguás, ' those pirates of the
Paraná, disdaining gods, destroying man,
staining their faces with the juice of the
caraguatá, a purple like that of Tyre ;
having a vulture's wing dependent from
their ears ; very hard of heart, and skilled
in paddling a canoe, and striking fish with
arrows, like themselves alone.'

Languages so hard as to appear impossible to Europeans, 'so do they snort and sneeze and cough their words,' had to be overcome ; speaking both Guaraní and Mocobío, 'with the Latin and some touch of Greek and Hebrew.' Though brought up as a priest, he had become a horseman ; riding with the Gauchos day and night, though, as he tells us, never quite so much at home upon a horse of Paraguay as on a horse of Europe ; for it appears 'a horse of Paraguay' (and this I have observed myself, though not a Jesuit) 'is apt to shy and bound, and if the bridle be neglected, lift his head up in the air, and, arching his back, give with his rider (*dar con el ginete*) on the ground.'

Medio chapeton[1] *el padre*, as I think I see.

This was the sort of training a Jesuit missionary underwent in Paraguay, and for which it may be that Salamanca, Rome, Coimbra, or even Paris, fitted him but moderately.

San Joaquin itself could not have been a place of residence to be called luxurious.

---

[1] *Chapeton* is used by Spanish Americans for a new-comer, and by inference a bad horseman.

Like all the Jesuit missions in Paraguay, it
must have been a little place built round a
square, enclosing a bright green lawn ; a
kind of island lost in the sea of forest. A
well-built church of stone in the Jesuit
style of architecture, the college with its
storerooms for hides and wool and maté.
On each side the church a date palm,
waving like a bulrush. A long low row
of wooden houses, with deep verandahs,
thatched with palm leaves. An air of calm
and rest and melancholy over the place, a sort
of feeling as if you had landed (and been
left) in Juan Fernandez. Sun and more sun,
heat and more heat, and a whitish vapour
stealing at evening time over the woods,
wrapping the town within its folds, and
giving the bell of the Angelus a muffled
sound.

In the daytime women, in white clothes,
with baskets on their heads of maize and
mandioca, hair like horses' tails cut square
across the forehead and hanging down their
backs, clustered like bees in the centre of
the square, and chattered Guaraní in under-
tones, like Indians always use. The men

in white duck trousers, barefooted, and with cloaks of red *bayéta*,[1] lounged about, doubtless when the Jesuits were not looking ; as they do to-day.

Before the houses, posts of heavy wood, to which from sunrise till sunset horses ready saddled stood fastened ; horses which seemed to sleep, unless an unwary passer-by approached too near them, when they sprang back into life, snorting with terror, sat back upon their *jáquimas*, causing their owners to leave their maté, and to bound like cats to quiet them, with cries of ' Jesus,' ' Ba eh picó,' and other things less fitting to record, even in Guaraní. Outside the town the forest stretching into distance. Forests of viraró, of urunday, tarumá, araguaý, and zamaú, of every strange and iron-hearted wood that Europe never hears of, even to-day. Trees which grow, and fall and rot, and spring up bound with lianas like thick cordage, and through which the bell-bird calls, the guacamayos flutter and tucanes dart ; and where the spotted tiger creeps (that Jesuit of the

[1] *Bayéta* is a kind of fine baize.

jungle) beside some pool covered with leaves of the Victoria Regia.

The college itself, no doubt a cheerless place enough, dazzling with whitewash on the outside, and in the interior dark and heavy, with an aroma of tobacco-smoke to serve as incense. For furniture a *catre* of wood, with strips of hide for bedstraps, or a white cotton hammock swung from an iron ring let into the beams. A shelf or two of books, chiefly on medicine or engineering or architecture ; for your Jesuit was doctor, music - master, architect, and sometimes military instructor to the community. Two or three chairs, roughly cut out of solid wood and seated with stamped leather in the Spanish style ; a table or two, a porous water-jar ; in the corner the padre's saddle on a trestle, and on a nail a gun ; for at times a Jesuit *capilla* became a place to fight as well as pray in.

In the forests scattered families of Indians lived, remnants of tribes destroyed by small-pox or by wars ; and it was the dream of every self-respecting, able-bodied Jesuit to find and mark these sheep wandering in the wilderness without a shepherd. What they underwent in hardships, lack of food, attacks of Indians, crossing swamps and rivers, by heat and cold, Guevara and Lozano, Ruiz Montoya and Father Dobrizhoffer, have set forth with pious pride, and more or less dog Latin.

News having come to San Joaquin that the trail of Indians had been crossed near to the town, he sallied forth, and having found and marked his sheep, compiled the following description, in which he tells, besides the story, what kind of man he was himself ; and proves beyond a doubt that, following the words of Santa Teresa, he ' was only fit for God.'

On the eve of the Evangelist Blessed St. John the Baptist, I took a guide and entered the Tarumensian woods accompanied by some neophytes. I crossed the Rio Empalado, and having carefully explored all the woods of the river Monday Miní, and discovering at length on the third day a human footstep, we tracked it to a little dwelling where an old woman with her son and daughter, a youth and maiden of fifteen and twenty years, were dwelling.

Being asked where the other Indians were to be found, the mother replied that no one dwelt in the woods but herself, her son and daughter, and that all the rest had died of small-pox.

Perceiving us doubtful as to the truth of this, the son said, 'You may believe my mother, for I have looked for a wife up and down these woods for leagues, but never met a human being.'

Nature had taught the young savage that it was not lawful to marry his sister.

I exhorted the mother to remove to my town, where she would be more comfortable.

She declared herself willing to do so, but there was one objection : 'I have,' she said, 'three peccaries which I have brought up. They follow us wherever we go, and I am afraid, if they are exposed to the sun in a dry plain, unshaded by trees, they will soon die.'

'Pray be no longer anxious,' I said ; 'I shall treat these dear little animals with due kindness. Lakes, rivers, and marshes will always be at hand to cool your favourites.'

Here I detect the cloven foot for the first and last time in this worthy man's career, for round San Joaquin there are no rivers or lakes, and I fear his anxiety to mark the sheep rendered him careless of the little peccaries.

Induced by these promises, she set out with us, and reached the town on the first of January.

No date is given, but I fancy in San

Joaquin time was what they had most to dispose of.

And now it will be proper to give an account of the dwelling of the mother and her children. Their hut consisted of the branches of the palm-tree and their drink of muddy water.

To this day the majority of huts in Paraguay are of palm-leaves, and for the muddy water, it grits yet (in dreams) between my teeth.

Fruits, antas,[1] rabbits and birds, maize and mandioca were their food, a cloth woven of the leaves of the caraguatá their bed and clothing. They delighted in honey, which abounds in the hollow trees. The smoke of tobacco the old woman inhaled day and night through a reed. The son constantly chewed tobacco-leaves. The youth wore a cloak of caraguatá,[2] reaching to the knees. The girl wore a short net by day, which she used as a hammock by night. This appearing to me too transparent, I gave her a cotton towel to cover her more effectually. The girl, folding up the towel,

---

[1] Tapirs.

[2] The Caraguatá is a plant of Bromeliaceæ. For all I know in the language of science (?), it may be 'hirsute,' 'imbricate,' and all the rest of the jargon called scientific. It resembles a pineapple in shape; only it is at least three times as large, and the inside of the leaves are bright red. It grows by the side of woods. It is used instead of hemp in Paraguay. The Indians of the Chaco call it chaguar.

put it on her head ; but at the desire of her mother wrapped herself in it. I gave the youth, too, some linen clothes to wrap himself in. Before putting on these he had climbed the trees, agile as a monkey, but his wrapper impeded him so that he could hardly move a step.

Whether my author thinks it an advantage that, of a happy climbing faun, he had made a being who could not move a step, I do not know. But 'all was conscience and tender heart' with him, for he observes immediately :

In such extreme need, in such penury, I found them, experiencing the rigours of the anchorites of old without discontent, vexation, or disease. The mother and son were tall and good-looking, but the daughter had so fine and elegant a countenance that a poet would have taken her for a nymph or dryad. She united a becoming cheerfulness with great courtesy, and did not seem at all alarmed at our arrival.

When one reads an account like this, and reflects that Cook, Cabeza de Vaca, de Bougainville, Columbus, and others, all unite in describing similar people ; and when one has even seen them oneself, it seems a pity that villainous saltpetre should have been digged, more villainous whisky distilled, and that Bible peddling should have become a trade.

As this insulated family had no intercourse with any but themselves, their Guaraní was much corrupted. The youth had never seen a woman but his mother and his sister. The girl had seen no man but her brother, her father having been torn to pieces by a tiger before she was born. Not to go unattended [*sin compañero*], she had a little parrot and a small monkey on her arm.

The new proselytes were quickly clothed in the town, and food supplied them.

L'ultimo lasso ! de' *lor* giorni allegri.

I also took care that they should take frequent excursions to the woods to enjoy the shade and pleasant freshness of the trees, to which they had been used, for we found by experience that savages removed to towns often waste away from the change of food and air, and from the heat of the sun, accustomed as they have been to moist, shady, and cool groves.

The same was the fate of the mother, son, and daughter.

One hardly knows whether to laugh or cry. Hamlet has put the folly of falling a-cursing in such a light that perhaps not to *raggionar* is best, but silently to pass.

A few months after their arrival they were afflicted with a heaviness and universal rheum (*reuma universal*), to which succeeded pains in the eyes and ears and deafness. Lowness of spirits and disgust to food at length wasted their strength to such a degree that an incurable consumption followed. After languishing some months the old mother, who had been properly instructed (one feels relieved) in the Christian religion and baptized, delivered up her spirit with a mind so calm, so acquiescent with the Divine will, that I cannot doubt but that she entered into a blessed immortality.

I would fain hope so too, so that at least the unhappy sufferer had some practical set-off against the clothes and baptism which were her apparent ruin.

The girl, who had entered the town full of health and beauty, soon lost all resemblance to herself. Enfeebled, withering by degrees like a flower, her bones hardly holding together, she followed her mother to the grave, and, if I be not deceived, to heaven.

Again I hope the good and worthy muddlehead was right in his conjecture, though there is no mention of baptism or religious instruction in this case.

The brother still surviving was attacked by the same malady, but being of a stronger constitution overcame it. The measles, which made great havoc in the town [another blessing in disguise], left him so confirmed in health that he seemed beyond danger. He was of a cheerful nature, went to church daily [*pobrecito*], learnt the doctrines of Christianity with diligence, was gentle and compliant to all, and in everything discovered marks of future excellence. Nevertheless, to put his perseverance to the proof, I thought best to delay his baptism. At this time a rich and Christian Indian [*un Indio rico y cristiano*], who at my request had received the catechumen into his house, came and said to me : 'Father (*pai*), our wood Indian is in perfect health of body, but is a little astray in mind. He makes no complaints, but says sleep has deserted him : his mother and sister appearing to him every night and saying, "Suffer thyself to be baptized." '

I wonder a little at this, when they knew how fatal baptism had proved in their own case.

'We shall return to take thee when thou dost not expect it.' This vision, he says, takes away his sleep. 'Tell him,' I answered, 'to be of good cheer, for that the melancholy remembrance of his mother and sister is the cause of his dreams, and they, as I think [O Pai Yponá, were you not certain then ?], are gone to heaven, and have nothing more to do with this world.'

A few days after the same Indian returned, giving the same account. Suspecting there was something in it, I hastened to the house, and found him sitting up in bed. On my asking for his health, he answered, 'I am well and free from pain,' but that he could not sleep, from the vision of his mother and sister telling him to be baptized, and saying they were ready for him. This he told me prevented him from getting any rest. I thought it probable that this was a mere dream, and worthy of neglect. Mindful, however, that dreams have often been Divine admonitions, and oracles of God, as appears from Holy Writ, it seemed advisable in a matter of such moment to consult the security and tranquillity of the catechumen. Being assured of his constancy and of his acquaintance with the chief heads of religion by previous interrogation [*interrogatorios previos*], I soon after baptized him by the name of Luis. This I did on the 23rd of June, the eve of St. John, about the hour of ten in the morning, by the sand clock.

On the evening of the same day, without a symptom of disease or apoplexy, he quietly expired.

This event, a fact well known to the whole town, and which I am ready to attest on oath, astonished every one.

I should have only looked on it as certain to occur after the fateful effects of the previous treatment (and *interrogatorios*) on the mother and sister.

7

I leave my reader to form his own opinion, but in my own mind I could never deem the circumstance merely accidental. I attributed it to the exceeding compassion of the Almighty that these three Indians were discovered by me in the recesses of the woods ; that they so promptly complied with my exhortations to enter my town and embrace Christianity, and that they closed their lives after receiving baptism. The remembrance of my expeditions to the Empalado, though attended by many dangers and hardships, is still most grateful to my heart ; insomuch as it proved highly fortunate to the three wood Indians, and advantageous to the Spaniards. These last having been certified by me that no more savages (*sic*) remained, collected many thousand pounds of yerba maté, from which they derived an amazing profit.

This much of the Guaraní town of Tarumá. If on this subject [says our pious author] I appear to have written too much, let the reader be told that I have passed over many remarkable things in silence.

The above history almost seems to show that there were Jesuits and Jesuits even in Paraguay.

Why has their rule, then, called forth such censure, and gained them such an evil reputation ? Why have both Catholics and Protestants combined to write them down ? It could not be their wealth in Paraguay,

for at their expulsion, when all their colleges were ransacked, only a small sum
was found. It could not be that the luxurious lives they led excited envy, for the
little episode I have commented on is but
one of many scattered through the lives of
all of them, and recorded in various tongues
from Latin to Guaraní. It may be that
the viceroys feared an *imperium in imperio*
in Paraguay ; though how some thousands
of such Indians as those who suffered
baptism and death in the old priest's story
could shake an empire is difficult to under-
stand. It may have been that the Mission
priests in Paraguay paid for the sins of
Jesuit intriguers at the Courts of Europe.
Theology does not, I think, reject vicarious
punishment. Certain it is that mention of
Paraguay and the Missions never fails to
call forth talk of despotism and tyranny,
and complaints of Indians turned to mere
machines by the too paternal government
of the Jesuits. This may have been so. It
may have been that their scheme of government would not have satisfied Sir Thomas
More, Karl Marx, or Plato. Still, there

were then Indians to govern. Where are they now? Where are the thirty towns, the 80,000 or 100,000 inhabitants, the flocks and herds, the domestic cattle ('with wild ones innumerable'), spoken of in the report of the suppression of the Missions, by Buccarelli, Viceroy to Charles the Third?

Where are the well-built churches, and the happy simple folk who worshipped in them, believing all things?

Take horse from Itapua, ride through San Cosme, the Estero-Neembucú, or San Ignacio Miní, and look for Indians, look for churches, look for cattle, or any sign of agriculture ; you will find all dead, gone, desolate, deserted, or fallen to ruin. Sleep in the deserted towns, and perhaps, as I did, camping in the plaza of La Trinidad alone, my horse tied to a tuft of grass beside me, you may see a tiger steal in the moonlight out of the deserted church, descend the steps, and glide into the forest.

Azara and Bonpland say that the communistic rule of the Society rendered the Indians thriftless and idle ; though this is

difficult to reconcile with their further state-
ment that they were well-nigh worked to
death. The Indians themselves were not
aggrieved at communism ; for, in their
petition to the Viceroy at the expulsion of
the Jesuits, they complain of 'liking not
the fashion of living of the Spaniards, in
which no man helps the other.' It may
have been that the Spanish settlers in
Paraguay wanted the Indians to slave for
them in their plantations, and that the
Jesuits withstood them. But when the ruin
of an institution or of an individual is
decreed, reasons are never wanting. The
Jesuits in Europe may have deserved their
fate. In Paraguay, in spite of writers none
of whom saw the Missions under their rule,
the Jesuits did much good, mixed with
some folly, as is incidental to mankind.

If only on the principle that a living dog
is of more value than a dead king, the
policy of isolation the Jesuits pursued was
not a bad one, for it left them at least
Indians to govern. Be all this as it may, I
have no doubt that many learned men,
skilled in the Greek and Latin (but not in

Guaraní), have written and will write of the
Jesuits in Paraguay, and prove to demon-
stration that it is fruit for self-congratulation
that the Indians of the Missions are free
and non-existent. Still, I sometimes wish
that I had seen the Missions full of Indians,
and stocked with cattle, instead of desolate
and fallen into decay. And for the amiable
and apostolic priest who told the story of
his labours in the Tarumensian wilds, and
chronicled in execrable Spanish the dis-
covery, death, and baptism of his three
victims, I have only one complaint to make,
and that is, that he did not tell us if town
life proved fatal to the three little peccaries.

R. B. C. G.

V

A JESUIT

IT was, I think, at the little port of the Esquina in Corrientes that he came on board. A priest at first sight, yet not quite similar to other priests, at least to those whose mission is only for mass and meat. A Spaniard, too, at first sight, with the clean-cut features of Old Castille, the bony hands that mark the man of action, and feet as square as boxes. Withal not commonplace, though unassuming, but with a look of that intensity of purpose which many saints have shared with bulldogs. All day the steamer had been running between the myriad islets of the Paraná. Sometimes it seemed impossible she could thread her way between the mass of floating *camalote* which clogged the channel.

Now and then the branches of the tall Lapachos and Urundays swept the deck as the vessel hugged the shore. On every side a mass of vegetation, feathery palms, horny mimosas, giant cacti, and all knotted together with lianas like cordage of a ship, stretching from tree to tree. The river, an enormous yellow flood, flowing between high banks of rich alluvial soil ever slipping with a dull splash into the stream. On every side Nature overwhelming man and making him feel his littleness.

Such a scene as Hulderico Schmidel, Alvar Nuñez, or Solis may have gazed on, with the exception that now and then wild horses came into sight and snorted as the steamer passed ; or a Gaucho, wilder than the horse he rode, with flowing hair and floating poncho, cantered along the plain where the banks were low, his *pingo* galloping like a piece of clockwork. In the slack water, under the lee of the islands, alligators lay like trunks of trees and basked. In the trees the monkeys and parrots chattered and howled, and *picaflores* flitted from flower to flower ; and once between the islands a tiger appeared swimming in pursuit of some *carpinchos*. The air was full of the filmy white filaments like cobwebs which the north wind always brings with it in those countries, and which clung from every rope and piece of rigging, making the steamer look as if she had run through a cotton manufactory. In every cabin mosquitoes hummed and made life miserable.

On board the steamer everything was modern of the modern, but modern seen through a Spanish medium—no door would shut, no bolt would draw, and nothing made to slide would work; engines from Barrow-in-Furness, or from Greenock, but the brass-plate which set forth the place of their manufacture was so covered with patina as to leave the name a matter of conjecture. The captain was from Barcelona, and fully impressed with the importance of his native province and city; the crew, Italians and Spanish Basques; the pilot, a Correntino, equally at home in the saddle or in a schooner, and knowing every turn and bend of the river in the nineteen hundred miles from Buenos Ayres to Cuyabá. The passengers, chiefly Bolivians and Brazilians, hating one another, but indistinguishable to the undiscerning foreigner ; an Argentine *tropero*, going to Corrientes ; a Spanish merchant or two from Buenos Ayres ; the ambulant troop of Italian opera singers, without which no river steamer in South America ever seems to leave a port ; a gambler or two in pursuit of their daily avocation ; some Paraguayans with innumerable children and servants, and birds in cages, all chattering in Guaraní, like the Christian Indians they are ; some English business men, looking as business-like as if in London. On the lower deck a group of Gauchos with their *capataz*. Seated all day long they played at 'Truco' with cards as greasy as bits of hide, and so well marked upon the back that the anxiety of the dealer to conceal their faces seemed a work of supererogation. These were the only passengers who thoroughly enjoyed themselves. Lounging on the deck when tired of playing cards, or when tobacco failed or maté was

unprocurable, they talked of horses and
scratched their marks upon the deck, to
the annoyance of the captain, with the
points of their *facones*. Had the voyage
endured a month they would not have
complained, so long as meal-times came in
regular succession and there was room to
stretch their *recados* upon the deck at
night to sleep. Mosquitoes troubled them
not, and though they never seemed to look
at anything, not a bend of the stream or a
tree, still less a horse, escaped their observa-
tion. If there was a guitar procurable, they
sang to it for hours in the moonlight, but
in such quiet fashion as to disturb no one,
least of all themselves. Their songs were
chiefly of melancholy love affairs or of the
prowess of famous horses. If the first-
class passengers danced upon the deck at
night, the Gauchos sauntered up and criti-
cised them, as if they had been cattle at
a *saladero*.

At the Esquina, the usual mild bustle
of a South American riverine port was soon
over. The captain of the port, after a full
hour's waiting, rode leisurely to the pier,

got off his horse, lighted his cigarette, and sauntered to his boat. The Italian boatmen were galvanised into a little life, and stood and grinned, and tried to look as if they were at Naples or at Genoa. After much talking of yellow fever and the perennial revolution, and inquiries if such and such a one had had his throat cut, the passengers surrendered themselves to be cheated by the boatmen and went ashore. As the vessel slid away and the little city baking like a white oven in the sun, with the Argentine flag with its bars of blue and white flapping against the flagstaff, and the horses tied to the *palenque* in front of the houses in the plaza, faded out of sight, our interest centred on the only passenger who had come aboard. Nobody knew him, and he did not seem to be a man of much importance. The stewards, observing that all his luggage consisted of a newspaper which he carried under his arm, turned from him with disdain. The traders and the gamblers saw he was not of them. Even the Gauchos looked a little scornful, and remarked that he was most probably a *maturango*. In their vocabulary *maturango*, meaning a bad rider, is the most contemptuous term of them all. Amongst them, a philosopher who touched his horse with his toe in mounting would have no acceptation. As for the itinerant opera company, even the basso (always the wit of an Italian opera troupe) had nothing to say about him.

Still, after a little time, and as the steamer skirted the city of Corrientes and entered the Paraguay, passing Humaitá with the church a ruin still from the time of the war, and left Curupaity behind her, passing into the regions of dense forests where the Bermejo and the Pilcomayo, after running through the Chaco, fall into the Paraguay, it was clear that the lonely passenger had become a favourite. Why, was not apparent at first sight. Certainly he knew the river better in some respects than the Correntino pilot, and could point out the various places where, in bygone times, such or such a missionary had met his fate by Indian spear or arrow. ' Just between that tuft of palms under the mountain in the distance, Father Julian Lizardi, a Biscayan, received his martyr's crown in 1735 at the hands of the Chiriguanás. Beside his body, pierced with arrows, was found his breviary open at the office for the dead, as if, poor soul, he had been trying to read his own funeral service. *In pace requiescat.* There, where you see the broken tower and ruined walls, the *tapera*, as they call it here in these countries, the Jesuits had a town amongst the Guaycurus. This was before the Philistines prevailed against them, and withdrew them from their work and light from the souls of the poor Indians.'

Thus discoursing and smoking cigarettes perpetually, for the newspaper contained nothing but paper and tobacco, he wound himself into our hearts. The traders swore by him; even the Englishmen, when he said he was a Jesuit, replied that they did not care, he was a damned good fellow, and he smiled, not understanding but seeing they were pleased. The Brazilians in the morning asked for his blessing on the sly, though all freethinkers when talking in the smoking-room. The opera troupe were his devoted slaves, and he used to sit and hear their grievances and settle their quarrels. Even the Gauchos, before they went ashore at Asuncion, chatted familiarly with him, and asked him if he knew the Pope, and told him of the 'deaths they owed,' and wondered if one of them who never was baptized and, therefore, had no saint, could go to heaven ; to which he answered : 'Yes, my son, on All Saints' Day.'

We left Asuncion with its towers and houses hidden in orange gardens, and the great palace, in the style of Palladio, by the river's edge. Asuncion, the capital of the viceroyalty of Paraguay—in the Spanish times a territory about as large as Europe, and now a sleepy semi-Indian village, after having endured the three successive tyrannies of Francia and the two Lopez—looks over the Chaco at the great desert, still an unknown wilderness of swamps and forests. Then the river narrows and all traces of civilisation are left behind. Here the Jesuit, for all had now begun to call him nothing else, seemed to brighten up as if he expected something, and his stories of the Jesuits of old times became more frequent. Little by little his own history came out, for he was not communicative, at least about himself. Near the Laguna de los Xarayes it appeared that the Company of Jesus had secretly started a mission amongst the Guasarapos, and he was of it. Never since the days of the Jesuits' glory in America had any missionary been bold enough to make the experiment. Fernandez and Alvar Nuñez, in times past, had written of their fierceness and intractability. Nuflo de Chaves, the bold adventurer, who founded the town of Sta. Cruz de la Sierra, had met his death close to their territory. At long intervals they had been known to come to the mission of El Santo Corazon, or sometimes to wander even as far as that of Reyes in the district of the Moxos, while throughout the region of the upper Paraguay stories of their outrages and murders were rife. In the long hot nights, as the vessel drew near to Corumbá, the passengers would sit and listen to the tales the Jesuit told. Seated

in a cane chair, dressed in rusty black, a
jipijapa hat, nothing about him priestly but
his breviary and *alzacuello*, without an
atom of pose, he held us spellbound. Even
the Catalonian captain, nurtured to show
his Liberalism by hating priests of all
degrees, Catholic and Protestant, grew
quite friendly with the 'little crow,' as he
called him, and promised to put him ashore
as near the mission as he could. 'Mission,
Señor Captain! there is no mission, that is,
now. I am the mission, that is, all that
now remains of it.'

Such was the case, for it appeared that
the Indians, either tired of missions or bored
by preaching, or because they wished to kill
a white man, had risen some months ago
and burnt the church and buildings, killed
the priests, with the exception of our passenger, and returned to wander in the
forests. 'Those who are dead are now in
glory,' our Jesuit observed, 'and the Indians
will find some other pastors more successful, though none more self-devoted.' Every
one on board the steamer protested, and the
little man smiled as he informed us that he

had escaped and made his way to a settlement, had gone to Buenos Ayres, whence he had telegraphed to Rome for orders, and the one word had come : ' Return.'

Next day, after much protestation from the captain, the steamer stopped at a sort of clearing in the forest, lowered a boat, and the Jesuit went ashore, his newspaper well filled with cigarettes. Stepping ashore, he stood for an instant, a little figure in rusty black, a midget against the giant trees, a speck against the giant vegetation. The steamer puffed and snorted, swung into the stream, the Jesuit waved his hand, took up his newspaper of cigarettes and, as the passengers and crew stood staring at him from the decks and rigging, walked into the forest.

R. B. C. G.

VI

RAS DOURA

A FUNERAL in fine weather has always seemed to me much more depressing than on the ordinary wet day which is generally associated with the function. It may be that the very rarity of a fine day in Great Britain makes it seem hard that the principal should be unable to enjoy it. Indeed there is a sort of feeling that the funeral cannot be a real one, in the same way as, on arriving at Naples, or any southern port on a fine day, one never fancies the people can die, or need suffer any hardships in life other than mosquitoes. Especially is this true of Northern Africa, where a violent death seems natural enough to all true believers ; but a funeral with mourners, tears and sham tears, black clothes, strong drinks, and all the pomp and circumstance of ignoble woe, seems out of place ; and when a Christian dies in Tunis or Morocco, it is as if the mourners were acting a comedy. It is said a funeral has a special attraction for all North Britons. Why this should be so I do not know. Certain it is that in this country a funeral is not an attractive ceremony. However, I suppose no man can ever quite be outside his nation, and I confess to a sort of interest in a funeral myself.

Between Larache and Rabat there is a chain of swampy lakes, haunted by ibises, flamingoes, and herons, and navigated by the natives in bales of bulrushes fastened into a sort of gondola with strips of hide. Just the sort of reedy swamp, with a white miasmatic vapour hanging over it, that used to be depicted in steel engravings in old books of African travels. The head of the chain of lakes is called Ras Doura. All along the lakes are little collections of huts—half village, half encampment—as if the Arabs who inhabit them were haunted with *saudades* (no English word renders

the Portuguese *saudade*) of the desert
from whence they come, and were afraid
to lose their individuality by building in
too permanent a fashion. In fact these
recollections persist amongst them in a
way to us quite unintelligible. Travelling
one day between Fez and Tangier, I asked
an Arab at an encampment where he and
his people came from. 'From the Nile,'
he answered. 'That seems far enough to
journey,' I rejoined ; 'when did you leave
it ? ' Said he, with the air of one who
states a commonplace, 'About six hundred
years ago.'

All these villages are dreary places,
situated on a strip of sandy soil between
the Atlantic and the chain of lakes.
Beyond the lakes are plains, on which
graze horses, camels, goats, and sheep,
tended by men who pass a life like that
passed in Chaldea and Palestine by the
authors of the Bible. In the distance are
three sacred white domes, the tombs of
saints. In Morocco every district has its
saint's tomb, and the traveller asks his way
from Sidi this to Sidi that, in the selfsame

way as a tramp in rural England steers his
course from the 'Chequers' to the 'Bells.'
All round the three white tombs is a burial
ground ; for where a saint is buried your
true believer likes to lay his bones.   Women
resort to them to gossip and to pray, and
to implore the saint to grant them children
who shall grow up horsemen and good
men at spear and gun.   Something about
your Moorish cemetery appeals to me.
Often it is a waste of lentisks, dwarf
rhododendrons, and arbutus, with lilies
and white cistus interspersed like stars in a
half-cloudy night.   Seldom there is a wall ;
and if there is one, it is generally built of
tapia (sun-dried mud), crumbling, and
with many breaches in it.   If there is no
wall, as is most usual, the cemetery lies open
to all passers-by ; on some of the graves
rough slabs of stone without inscriptions
stand up, others are quite flat, and some
stuck edgeways in the ground.   A goat or
two, or a black curly lamb, is always graz-
ing there, and paths in all directions cut it
into patterns.   It is not the place to ride
across in the dark without a shiver, and

yet, by a sort of attraction, you are sure to
find yourself with a tired horse at night
galloping amongst the graves on the outskirts of the town. There is nothing to
do on such an occasion but give your horse
his head, reflect that those whose graves
you ride upon have been bold riders to a
man, and trust in Allah.

The little village at Ras Doura looks
like a colony of bees. Not that the people
work an atom more than just to keep themselves from starving. In all Morocco no
man can be found so foolish as to say he
likes to work, far less to labour, except
under the pressure of hunger or of his
superiors. The likeness to a colony of
bees is purely esoteric. The huts are
circular on a sort of *fond de jupe* of
wicker-work with rushes. They finish in
a point, just like the beehives in an English
cottage garden—I mean the kind before
the patent wooden and glass inventions,
which I feel quite sure the bees detest,
came into vogue. The doors, for the
convenience of keeping the huts dry, and
for preventing hens, pigs, dogs, and other

small mammalia from coming in, are placed
about a yard above the ground, and measure but three feet in all in height, so that
the spectacle of a fat muslin-swathed sherif
struggling to emerge from one of them is
comical enough. Round about every bee-
hive stands a hedge of prickly bushes, cut
by the women in autumn and left to dry.
The Christian should not tie his horse to
them or touch them, any more than he
should fasten his reins to an area-railing or
a knocker in England. In the centre of
the village may be found a little square
building thatched with reeds, resembling
either a boathouse on Virginia Water or
a crofter's cottage in Harris or Benbecula.
This is the mosque where travellers sleep,
and whence the call to prayer arises five
times every day. Christians may no more
enter it than if it were the Khutubich at
Marakish or Muley Edris at Fez. It is
as sacred in its way as either of them.
But though so sacred, yet it is homelike
as a church in Iceland or in Spain; not
that, as far as I know, wayfarers ever sleep
in Spanish churches, although they do so

to this day in churches in Iceland—of course
at night, not at matins or at evensong. No
one ever saw a mosque locked up so that
the faithful could not enter it. By night
and day the doors are open (in Morocco),
and it always seems to me, after returning
from there, that the Christian church with
its padlock and its door seems churlish in
comparison. Surely to the true believer,
Christian or Mohammedan, the door of the
sanctuary never should be closed.

Over the village rests an air of listless
self-content—content that comes from the
sun and the possession of a horse or two,
tempered only by fleas, and the thought
that the Basha may be expected at any
moment. Yellow ulcerous dogs, that
shrink before the stick descends, may
be seen on every side, thin cows and
mangy camels, and before the house almost
certainly a horse, tied to a post as on
the Pampas, blinking in the sun, with a
high red saddle and a long gun hanging
from the pommel. No inhabitant is much
richer than his fellow, except perhaps the
omnipresent sherif, without whose presence

no village is complete. If all sherifs descend from Mohammed, his family must have been as reproductive as the families of the Norman knights who fought at Hastings, from whom all self-respecting Englishmen claim their descent. Still they fulfil a function in Morocco, being a sort of Levite class, in whom is vested the traditions of the race.

There is poverty, of course, in every Arab village, and plenty of it ; but not the poverty we know in Europe, and which we talk about and ponder on, and use for purposes of politics or religion, and by means of which we think to save our souls. Often no one has enough to eat, but no one dies of hunger. The race, in spite of want of food, is famous for beauty ; the men are active, tall, and strong, the women almond-eyed and swaying in their walk like ' oleanders by the water-courses when the south wind blows.' Marriage to an Arab villager is the key to the position. If he is married enough, his path is easy. One wife is poverty—only one pair of hands to work for you ; two wives, a

little better; three, respectability; four,
the happy consummation arrived at when
a man does nothing but mount his horse
at evening time and canter to the saint's
tomb, to chat and pray, join in the
'powder play,' or, better still, sit in
his garden thinking of nothing. Women,
of course, have rights according to the
Koran, but of a different nature to those
dreamed of by women who claim such
things in England. Each class of right
is, no doubt, the best for the country it
arose in.

There is nothing in life to make existence
either lively or unbearable in the village at
Ras Doura. Hardly any politics, no news,
but little scandal, no promiscuous visiting,
as no one, not the Sultan himself, can enter
any other person's house without his leave.
Nothing but stealing women and horses,
with gazelle-hunting and bustard-shooting,
in the way of field-sports; and for their
mental exercise, the practice, in all its
details, of their religion. Strange as it
may appear, in Morocco, and generally
in the East, no ridicule attaches to the

practice of one's faith. That which a man believes, he is not ashamed to do, even in public. Middle-aged men with beards dyed red with henna fall down and pray in public, and no one thinks them mad. They rise and talk of bullocks and of horses, of money and of women, the moment after, and no one thinks them hypocrites. In fact it is the fashion (just as in London or in Paris at the present time) to be religious. Your irreligious man, who does not pray at proper hours, omits to say Inshallah when he speaks of future things, who does not wash when washing is prescribed, and eats in Ramazan, is looked on as a *bourgeois*.

Still, even in Ras Doura, life has some excitements. At times the Zimouris issue from the forest of Mamora and drive off cattle in the night and carry away the girls. Then all the young men get to horse, and gallop to and fro, firing their guns, and swearing what they intend to do. Sometimes, of course, if the Zimouri *razzia* is a small one, they get their cattle or horses back, the girls more rarely; but

in general, as when a cry of 'Stop thief!'
echoes down a street, each passer-by is
eager to repeat it, but leaves the thief
alone. At other times the fighting is
serious enough, and the fighters fight the
better as they know the vanquished will
receive no quarter.

Occasionally a Sultan dies, and then
ensues a pleasant time of anarchy, in
which, if you be young and own a horse
and gun, you sally forth and join yourself to others of the proper sort, and
slay, burn, ravish, and steal horses, in the
selfsame way as these pastimes are so
graphically described in the Old Testament. Then, too, there are the feasts, as
the Mulud, the birthday of Mohammed,
which corresponds to our Nativity. Close
to Ras Doura is held the feast of Muley
Busalham, the patron of the riders. There,
mounted on their best, their *creditos*, as
the Gauchos of the Pampas say, seated on
saddles of white and green and eau de
Nil coffee, with orange-coloured silks,
with *haiks* and *selhams* flying in the air,
the horsemen for miles around are trysted

to 'play powder.' The 'powder play' (Lab el Barod) is the great diversion of all Eastern horsemen. Europeans think it foolish because they seldom try it themselves. In the same way, no doubt, a Maroqui would think a game of polo quite beneath contempt. To 'play the powder' on a fresh horse, amongst a mob of horsemen, on rough ground, to stand in the saddle and twist a heavy silver-mounted gun about one's head, wants practice. Only theologians are as intolerant as horsemen : 'no one can be saved but professors of my faith, but members of my church ; and even of my church but few are certain of salvation.' In the same way, no men can ride but Mexicans, Australians, Cossacks, Englishmen, Arabs, Hungarians, and Gauchos, and if you belong to any of those peoples, few but you yourself have ever really mastered the higher branches of the mystery. Then comes along a blue-eyed, flaxen-haired native of Iceland, on his little pony, and flies across a field of jagged lava, and leaves you sore amazed ; and so, perhaps, in the spiritual field, a man of no profession of faith, who never learnt a creed or a catechism, may enter paradise when clergymen lie howling.

Seated in my tent outside the village, watching the horses feed, and wondering if, after all, it was really worth while ever to return to England, I heard a wail. Like the Celtic *coronach* the Arab wail is something outside humanity. No jackal or coyote can produce a sound more dismal. It makes you sad at once, and yet sadness must be a kind of mental convention after all, for both the *coronach* and the Arab cry are just as doleful when they issue from the lips of a professional mourner. Fancy a mute at a funeral impressing one with sadness, or inducing thoughts of anything but gin and water. At the door of a little hut appeared a woman scarcely veiled, her hair streaming like a pony's tail. After her another, and then a group of children, all raising the same doleful cry. Then from the other beehives and huts came groups of women, to comfort and to wail in concert; in the midst the widow,

with tears running down her cheeks, and
striking her nails into her arms and breast.
The night before a horse had fallen on her
husband and killed him. The sorrow that
is dumb is not for Arabs ; the reserve of
power we hear so much of, and which makes
our grief, our joy, our eloquence, our acting
seem so unreal to all except ourselves, is not
for those who see the sun. ' Eyes of my
soul, how lightly didst thou ride over the
desert. True was thy aim at the enemies
of the Prophet. Generous thou wast and
noble. Protector of the poor, stay of the
childless, father of the downtrodden. How
shall I forget thee, life of my life ! ' Most
likely the horseman had never ridden except
to market on a stumbling, spavined horse,
or fired a shot except at wild duck in his
life ; and as to being generous or noble,
these are but merely terms of comparison.
Still, in an epitaph (in Latin, so that
the common people may not read it),
even in England, you occasionally see
apocryphal virtues set forth. Be that as
it may, the tears, the grief, the utter
self-annihilation were as touching as if

the tears had filtered through a cambric, hemstitched pocket-handkerchief.

Burial in Morocco follows hard upon the heels of death. The climate makes waiting impossible, and as a coffin is seldom or never used, there is no reason for delay. Wrapped in a clean white *haik*, strapped to a board, the feet sticking out stiffly in the pathetic and half-comic way that dead feet have, the dead man's body was brought to his own door. Before the tent a flea-bitten old grey mare with a little foal was feeding. A ragged boy, with a piece of camel's-hair rope, went up and caught and saddled her, and then the body was strapped upon her back face upwards, the foal watching the proceedings most intently. The burst of lamentation broke out louder than before, the wife appearing distraught with grief, the children standing stupid with the effect of weeping. The women led the widow to the house, the men formed in procession, with one leading the mare in front.

They passed along the lakes, waded a stream, a horseman every now and then firing a shot, the mare looking round anxiously. As they rode across the hill and vanished out of sight, the little foal whinnied and galloped after them, an unconscious mourner.

R. B. C. G.

VII

EL BABOR

At times in the East, the horror of the West, with all its factories, its hurry and its smoke, its frauds and charities, and life rendered so complex with infinities of nothingnesses, falls out of recollection at the actual horror of what is present. Before one's eyes appear the mud, the dust, the heaps of garbage rotting in the sun ; the scrofulous, the leprous folk seem, with the halt and maimed, to comprise mankind. The fleas, the lice, the dirt, the stench seem to be all-devouring. The ulcerous yellow dogs, who shrink away before the stick is even raised, give one a feeling of repulsion. On every side appears injustice, not alone the injustice that is coeval with life itself, but absolute injustice crying in the

streets—no man regarding it; even perhaps
applauding.

Then the thought arises if machinery
were introduced things might amend. At
least the wretched mules and donkeys
might find their hell a little cooler. The
camels might perhaps suffer less rope-galls,
and generally resemble a little less decayed
hair trunks; the women turning the stones
to crush the corn be not so old at twenty,
and when one was taken the other not so
much inclined to cry, ' Why was I left to
suffer ? ' At times one thinks so in despair,
when the flies rise in their myriads from
a dead horse or camel, and settle in the
corners of the beggars' eyes, on the scald-
heads of the children, or on the sores in
the horses' backs. Then comes a vision of
a neat steam-mill, with corrugated iron roof,
and greasy honest engineer with a handful
of cotton waste, wiping his face. His wife
with figure like a yard of water, lank and
elliptic in her cotton gown; the children
with their flaxen heads, rude manners, and
dirty noses; even the house with its furniture of two-carat mahogany, and ponderous

Bible, falsely called a polyglot (always wide
open for advertisement), become almost
agreeable by comparison. Even at times
when jogging across the sands, or plough-
ing through the mud, a railway with its
dust and clatter, clinker in your eye, lost
luggage, insolent ticket clerks, and offal
sandwich at the so-called refreshment-room,
appears a thing to be desired.

Thus moralising (and physical fatigue
conduces to philosophy), it seems to stand
to reason that if a man can do in a day
that which it takes a horse three days, a
camel a week, to do, that something, as
well as time, is saved. Then comes the
totting up of the pros and cons, the
balancing of conjectures, so dear to fools
and public men, one with another. If in
one province grain is rotting in the fields
and in another is worth five dollars the
almud, and folk are starving, and yet
the superfluity cannot repair the famine
for cost of carriage, the railway would be a
blessing. Let us, then, introduce it ; let
us have the switchback too, the bicycle, and
turnip dibble, and all will prosper. What

a reformer even the most conservative of Westerns is in the East, or anywhere, in fact, away from home! Not that in the East there is not much to reform, both in the temporal and the spiritual domain.

Mohammed, when he walked behind his camels, looking, no doubt, not very much unlike other Mohammeds of his and of our own time, and thinking of the time when somebody besides Ayesha would believe in him, never thought of saints or saints' tombs. Yet from Mecca to Agadhir, from Cairo to Candahar, the land is full of them. Perhaps the worship of St. Peter's, Eaton Square, might not seem ideal to the Syrian hegemonist. However, be that as it may, the name Mohammed is borne to-day by full three Arabs out of five. Where but in Spain do you find a Christian called Jesus? Familiarity, you say, ensures contempt. It may be so, but when the founder of a faith is not for ever in the faithful's mind or on his lips, the faith begins to languish. The real test of all religions is the material condition of the faithful. So, perhaps, Mohammed might just as well have driven his camels to the end, and never troubled himself about humanity. Idols are so consoling to the world.

Material condition of the faithful. What a base view! Is not the assurance that all mankind is damned except oneself and brother fetish worshipper enough? Well, that I leave to true believers, Mohammedan or otherwise. The difference between the kind who fardels bear and grunt and sweat under the burden of their lives appears to be a difference only of degree, whether the prophet is of Mecca or Jerusalem. If we in England shoot, when in the mood, a miner or two to encourage industry, in Morocco the Sultan eats up a whole village. The Christian works long hours, and is a bondsman to his trade, the Moor can never call his life his own; and so they ripe and rot respectively.

After a long day's march nothing is more impressive than suddenly to see the town you have begun to think is non-existent appear before you. Up it rises on a rocky hill, or on a cliff over the sea, like a town in the pages of a missal. On every side a waste of sand, a sea of grass, or wilderness of forest, and the town a thing apart, mysterious and wall-girt. Most Arab towns have a generic look to Western eyes, as I suppose Chemnitz and Blackpool would seem alike to Arabs. No blending of sky and houses, no cloud of smoke, no distant murmur, scarcely an indication that a town is near. Only the tracks which form the roads get broken and zigzag, in and out, like points at Clapham Junction ; donkeys and camels wander about looking for grass or orange-peel, dogs, and more dogs, and then the road leads through the gardens.

A garden in the East is not exclusively a place for flowers, nor yet for slugs and gardeners, gravel and mowing-machines, but generally a sort of unkempt paradise, hedged in with aloes. An unkempt paradise of palms and orange-trees, figs and pomegranates, patches of canes all waving in the air like dulse in the slack-water on a beach, grass studded with lilies, clover, and narcissus, a *noria*[1] in the

---

[1] *Noria* is the Arabic *hansah*, the wheel with earthenware jars on it, which, turned by a camel, woman, bullock, or donkey, brings up water in sufficient quantity for Spanish or Eastern wants.

middle, and at the entrance two inconsequent
white gate-posts, with a broken bullock
cart to serve as gate. Everywhere a sound
of water running in little channels of
cement. Still a garden, according to the
Eastern tastes, and pleasant to come to of
an evening, ambling on one's mule, and sit
with a Koran open before one and not to
read it, but doze till the hour of prayer.

Then the town with its walls and
battlements, on which the chattering storks
are sentinels, the steep approach, and the
gate with its horseshoe arch—the whole
standing against the sky as if cut out of
cardboard. The embrasures for cannon in
the walls grow green with moss and over-
grown with lentisks, palmitos, and white
alyssum, and through which peer carronades
left by the Spaniards or the Portuguese
in the times of their glory, with snakes
carved round the touch-holes, and the
legend ' Viva España,' ' Sov de un Dueño,'
and the date of the reign of the Catholic
King of the time of their manufacture.
The fortifications built by some Spanish
Vauban of those days, with many bastions

and ravelines and counterscarps and other
marvels of the art, now become obsolete,
and with the angles of the walls sharp as
the bow of a torpedo-boat. All around,
the moat now dry, and turned into a garden
for cabbages, *pimientos*, and *berengenas*,[1]
though in its time a defence for the town
against the infidel, as in the days when
Don Sebastian's army took refuge in it
after the battle at Alcazar el Kebir. Inside,
the usual Arab streets, slippery with filth,
strewn with intestines of sheep and fowls,
with rotten eggs and fruit, and set with
pebbles fitter to pave hell with than all the
good intentions forgotten since the Deluge.
Crowds of men in dusky white, with hoods
like Capuchins. Merchants in little stalls,
sitting, like josses in a temple, at the receipt
of custom and never finding any, and yet
just as contented as if they dealt in
thousands. Men jostling past as if the
fate of empires depended on their reaching
the beach with their load of refuse in a

---

[1] *Berengena* is the egg plant. It has always been a favourite
vegetable with the Moors. Before the expulsion of the Moriscos
from Spain, it was a saying in reference to the abundance of anything, ' As plentiful as *berengenas* in a Morisco's garden.'

given time. Camels pass by swaying like
vessels at an anchorage. Blind men, lepers,
and madmen, whom we seclude in mad-
houses (and parliaments) ostensibly to do
them good, but really to spare our feelings
the shock of seeing how little difference
there is between us, roam the streets or sit
serenely in the sun, hunting for lice. A
square arcaded plaza where corn is sold,
and where soft soap, oranges, and spices,
and the futile things which form the staple
of the commerce of the East, change hands.
Houses white and red and chocolate, pale
yellow, and light blue, with doors hermetically
sealed, and of which the master carries the
key (eight inches long) stuck in his waist-
band when he sallies forth to cheat or pray,
give an air of unreality to everything. Under
the arches, the merchant cheats his customer
with false weights, and the customer imposes
(when he can) bad copper money on the
merchant by the sackful. All passes in full
light of day, and neither is ashamed.

The mosque towers, slender like stalks
of cat mace, rise into the clear sky. The
Marsa (port) at which barges unload and

towards which a stream of laden donkeys is always staggering, and where a sallow Maltese or Gibraltarian (Consul for all the nations under heaven) lounges and ticks off nothings in a note-book ; then a tidal river with a bar harbour, where the ribs and keels of ships which once were pirate galleys from Sallee lie bleaching. An Arab town, in fact, just like another, with all its horrors to the ear and nose, and beauty to the eyes, but with a notable exception. Just outside the walls an open space of sand, where caravans have camped for centuries, a mangy plot of grass or two, on which women sell firewood, and where grave men walk up and down holding each other's hands like little children. On one side a height looking down on a shipless sea, defended by a battery, in which the cannon lie rusty amongst the ruins of their carriages ; and on the other side the notable exception. Hard by a little grove of fig-trees, an enterprising Spaniard has started a corn-mill, in its neat tin shed with corrugated iron roof, as hideous as if in England or Massachusetts. All day

long the wheezy high (or low) pressure
engine puffs, and sends a jet of steam into
the air. It is the *babor*, such being the
way the Spanish word *vapor* issues from
Arab lips. As it puffs and wheezes the
sun seems to die out, and an air of Hartle-
pool or Greenock overspreads the place.
Like the creature Burns saw on the lady's
bonnet in church, it fixes the attention
upon itself—Arabs, camels, women in their
shroud-like robes, Jewesses with unstable
busts and hair like horses'-tails, dressed in
the crudest of crude colours, and still not
without attraction, grave riders on their
fiery horses, with pasterns dyed with henna,
pass and one does not see them. As in
an exhibition, the Whistlers, Sargents,
Laverys, and Guthries pass unperceived,
and one cannot tear oneself away from
some outrage by a Royal Academician.

Machinery of every kind is awe-inspiring
to the Oriental mind, from a watch to a
phonograph all is 'Shaitanieh,' a devil's
trick, a thing past comprehension. Even
to some of us not born Orientals, the way
a key turns in a lock, or how the sucker

in a pump raises the water, is a thing which, like faith or baptism, we take on trust from our elders without inquiry. I remember (here 'I enter on the scene in person') talking with some Arabs of the villainy of governments,—the staple topic of conversation in lands where no one is so foolish as to think his rulers love him. A man took up his parable and said, 'In Algeria, I believe, the Government does really love the people.' All were incredulous, myself among the rest, or more than all the rest. 'I happened to be in Constantine,' he said, 'at the fête of the Republic.' How is it in a Republic they have no Sultan? . . . 'On the first day there were the races, horses ran fleeter than gazelles, and on them were seated little English devil-boys, ugly as Ginûn, and dressed in parti-coloured clothes. In the evening there were fireworks, then a ballet, at which 200 Christian girls, each one well worth 500 dollars, danced with hardly any clothes on. Next day was best of all, for early in the morning the soldiers brought a man out into the public square, and then before us all they cut his head off with a machine.' I agreed that French philanthropy could go no further.

All things must begin slowly, and if a railway or a steam merry-go-round were not attainable, a corn-mill (or guillotine) was at least a step towards progress.

The owner of the mill, a Catalan from Reus, stood at the door. The kind of man able and willing to drive a nail into a wall with his head, or draw it with his teeth. His costume neat and civilised ; trousers of bed-ticking, a dirty shirt held up at the wrist with elastic bands, a necktie with a pin of malachite, a greasy *boina*[1] upon his head, and *alpargatas*[2] on his naked feet. Spitting through his teeth he said in the sweet dialect of Catalonia (I omit his garnishing) : 'The Arabs are a lazy lot, liars and shirkers from their birth, and thievish as the mother of the devils. Here in this miserable place' (he came from Reus) 'I try to show the sons of dogs the way to progress and to civilisation.

[1] *Boina* is the Basque cap.
[2] *Alpargatas* are sandals made of canvas, with hemp soles.

Mother of God! you would scarcely credit it, I cannot get the swine to work more than six hours a day. In Catalonia every man works twelve at least, and women work fourteen.' I ventured to remark that the climates were different, and the people, and then insinuated, 'Surely you make a lot of money?' 'Money, Barajo, not more than 7 per cent upon my capital, and what is that to live among such heathens?' Resignedly I looked into the mill.

The day was hot, the temperature some 90 in the shade. Inside the mill, in a cloud of flour and dust, sweat trickling down their naked shoulders, I saw some Arabs hurrying about feeding the hoppers and carrying sacks of flour. They told me (also with garnishing) that the Catalonian had advanced them money or they would not work another minute: capital and labour. 'Hurry,' they said, 'was made for devils in hell and not for men and true believers, and here we hurry all the time.' 'Only six hours a day, my friends,' I said, 'and Christians work ten hours and twelve, and pass their lives dreaming of an illusive eight-hours day.' 'Christians are sons of " —— " '—well, the word was not a pleasing one—'little it matters to us how long they work, if they are fools enough.' 'Look, too,' I ventured, 'how fine the flour is ground, how quickly and how cleanly.' They answered, 'We eat none of it ; before this mill was built sometimes we worked all day, but then we stopped at intervals and talked and smoked, and even slept ; now all is changed, and this cursed " Babor " is our master, and while the wheels turn round we stand and minister.' 'Minister' was good, but still, if the men spoke truth, perhaps there is a glory of the sun, another of the snow. It may be that a *haik* looks ugly patched with broadcloth. Not to generalise too much, and not forgetting that in Morocco there are no Factory Acts, no County Council, and no busybodies who, leaving their own affairs to ruin, rove like Don Quixote about the land to smooth out other people's wrinkles, still the first essay I saw of bringing Western methods to the East was not too reassuring.   R. B. C. G.

VIII

THE HORSES OF THE PAMPAS

An Argentine friend of mine (old style)
wrote to me the other day from Paris :—

> I know you will think me a barbarian [I did
> not], but this Paris, this exhibition, this hurrying
> to and fro, this Eiffel Tower which I had to go up,
> have bored me dreadfully.
>
> Strange, too, that on the Pampas, as I read
> Daudet, the Goncourts, and Zola, it seemed so
> interesting to me. Now, I would give it all for an
> hour's gallop in my own country.

It was perhaps this letter (on which
my friend, to show his contempt of our
civilisation, had affixed no stamp) that set
me thinking of horses in general and of
the horses of the Pampas in particular.

Thus thinking, the thoughts of the
Eight Hours Bill on which you asked me

to write became vaguer and dimmer.
Therefore (a Scotchman must have his
therefore) I send you these rambling and
incoherent reminiscences of a life I have
lived, of men I have known, and of horses
that have been to me what horses never
can be to a man who surveys them through
the eyes of his stud groom.

Short-tailed, long-tailed, in cart or
carriage, ridden by 'Arry or by Lord
Henry, the horse of Europe (excepting
always the coster's pony) delights me not,
or very little. He seems to me a species
of property, a sort of investment for capital,
precarious sometimes, an unsatisfactory one
too often.

Is he ill, his malady must be ministered
to in the shape of beer to his groom ; does
he die, my equine investment is lost ; I must
try another.

On the Pampas it is different. He is
part of me, I live on him, and with him ;
he forms my chiefest subject of conversation, he is my best friend, more constant
far than man, and far exceeding woman.

What wonder, therefore, that my friend's

letter brought back to me the broad plains, the countless herds of horses, the wild life, the camp fire, the thousand accidents that make life alike so fascinating and so fatiguing in the desert.

Most people know that there are great plains called Pampas. Books of travel more or less authentic have informed them that these are roamed over by countless herds of horses.

As to what these horses are like, where they come from, and if there are any special peculiarities that distinguish them from other horses, few have inquired.

It seems to me that there are certain differences between the horses of Spanish America and the horses of any other country.

That they should more or less resemble those of the south of Spain, from whence they came, is nothing to be wondered at. That special conditions of food, climate, and surroundings should have produced a special type, is nothing extraordinary.

What, then, are the general characteristics of these horses?

That which specially attracts the attention of all those who see them for the first time is the great difference to be observed betwixt them when in motion and at rest. Saddled with the *recado*, the American adaptation of the Moorish *enjalma*; the heavy bed on horseback, with its semi-Moorish trappings; standing patiently before the door of some Gaucho's house from morn till sunset, they appear the most indolent of the equine race. But let the owner of the house approach with his waving poncho, his ringing spurs, his heavy hide and silver-mounted whip, and his long, flying black hair; let him by that mysterious process, seemingly an action of the will, and known only to the Gaucho, transfer himself to their backs, without apparent physical exertion, and all is changed. The dull, blinking animal wakes into life, and in a few minutes his slow gallop, regular as clockwork, has made him and his half-savage rider a mere speck upon the horizon.

In a country where a good horse costs a Spanish ounce (£3 : 15s.) it is not wonderful that all can ride, and all ride well. In a country where if you see a man upon a plain, you are always certain that it will be a man on horseback ; in a country where the great stock-owners count their *caballadas* by the thousand (Urquiza, the tyrant of Entre Rios, had about 180,000 horses), it is to be supposed that much equine lore, 'hoss sense' the Texans call it, has grown up. It is to be looked for that a special style of riding has arisen, as that, what we in Europe think strange is there regarded as an ordinary occurrence of every-day life.

It would indeed be as impossible to measure the Pampas horse by the standard of an English horse as to measure a Gaucho by the standard of an ordinary city man. Each man and each animal must be estimated according to the work he is required to do. Putting aside cart horses and those employed in heavy draught, almost every horse in England, except the cab horse, is an object of luxury. He has a man to look after him, is fed regularly, is never called on to endure great fatigue, carry much weight, still less to resist the inclemency of the weather. He is valued for his speed, for his docility, or merely for his pecuniary value in the market. In the Pampas none of these things is of prime importance. We do not require great speed from our horses, we care nothing as to their docility, and their pecuniary value is small. What we do look for is endurance, easy paces, sobriety, and power of withstanding hunger and thirst. A horse that will carry a heavy man seventy miles is a good horse, one that can do ninety miles with the same weight is a better horse, and if he can repeat the performance two or three days in succession, he is the best, no matter if he be piebald, skewbald, one-eyed, cow-houghed, oyster-footed, or has as many blemishes as Petruchio's own mustang.

Talking with some Gauchos, seated on the gravel, one starlit night, before a fire of bones and dried thistles, the conversation fell as usual upon horses. After much of the respective merits of English and Argentine horses, after many of the legends as closely trenching on the supernatural as is

befitting the dignity of horsemen in all
countries, an ancient, shrivelled Gaucho
turned to me with, 'How often do you
feed your horses, Don Roberto, in
England? Every day?' Thereupon, on
being answered, he said, with the mingled
sensitiveness and fatuity of the mixed race
of Spanish and Indian, 'God knows, the
Argentine horse is a good horse, the second
day without food or water, and if not He,
why then the devil, for he is very old.' In
all countries the intelligent are aware that
you cannot estimate a horse's goodness by
his stature. The average stature of the
Pampas horse is about $14\frac{1}{2}$ hands—what
we should call a pony in England. In
his case, however, his length of loin, his
lean neck, and relatively immense stride,
show that it is no pony we have to deal
with, but a horse, of low stature if you
will, but one that wants a man to ride him.

Intelligent and fiery eyes, clean legs,
round feet, and well-set sloping shoulders,
long pasterns, and silky manes and tails,
form the best points of the Pampas horse.
His defects are generally slack loins and

heavy head, not the 'coarse' head of the underbred horse of Europe, but one curiously developed that may or may not be, as Darwin says it is, the result of having to exert more mental effort than the horse of civilisation.

Of his colour, variable is he; brown, black, bay, chestnut, piebald, and gray, making a kaleidoscopic picture as on the dusky plains or through the green *monte* (wood) a herd of them flash past, with waving tails and manes, pursued by Gauchos as wild and fiery-eyed as they. As on the steppes of Russia, the plains of Queensland and Arabia, the trot is unknown. To cross a Pampa loaded with the necessaries of desert life, without a path to follow, it would be a useless pace. The slow gallop and the jogtrot, the Paso Castellano of the Spaniards, the Rhakran of the Turks, is the usual pace. The pacer of the North American, the ambler of the Middle Ages, is in little esteem upon the Pampas. You spur him, he does not bound; he is a bad swimmer. As the Gaucho says, 'he is useless for the lazo,

though perhaps he may do for an Englishman to ride.' 'Manso como para un Ingles'
(tame enough for an Englishman to ride)
is a saying in the Argentine Republic.

Where did these horses come from,
from whence their special powers of endurance? How did these special paces first
characterise them, and how is it that so
many of the superstitions connected with
them are also to be found amongst the
Arabs? My answer is unhesitatingly,
From the Arabs. All the characteristics
of the Arabs are to be observed in the
Argentine horses; the bit used is that of
Turkey and Morocco, the saddle is a
modification of the Oriental one, and the
horses, I think, are in like manner
descended from those in Barbary.

It is pretty generally known that the
conquest of America was rendered much
easier to the Spaniards by the fact that
they possessed horses, and the natives had
never seen them.

Great, well-watered, grassy plains, a fine
climate, and an almost entire absence of wild
beasts — what wonder, therefore, that the

progeny of the Spanish cavalry horses has extended itself (in the same way as did the horses turned loose at the siege of Azov in the sixteenth century on the steppes of Russia) all over the Pampas, from the semi-tropical plains of Tucuman and Rioja right down to the Straits of Magellan? Spanish writers tell us that Cordoba was the place from which the conquerors of America took most of their horses. To ride like a Cordobese was in the Middle Ages a saying in Spain, and such it has remained unto this day. Cervantes makes one of his characters say 'he could ride as well as the best Cordobese or Mexican,' proving the enormous increase of horses in the New World even in his time, not much more than a hundred years after the Conquest. In the plains of Cordoba, to this day, large quantities of horses are bred, but of a very different stamp from their descendants of the Pampas. Whence then did the original stock come from? Cordoba was the richest of the Moorish kingdoms of Spain in the thirteenth century. It was directly in communication with Damascus. Thus there is little doubt that the Cordobese horses were greatly improved by the introduction of the Arab blood. However, Damascus was a long way off, and the journey a difficult and a dangerous one. It therefore seems more probable to me that the most of the Cordobese horses came over from Barbary. A remarkable physical fact would seem to bear out my belief. Most horses, in fact almost all breeds of horses, have six lumbar vertebræ. A most careful observer, the late Edward Losson, a professor in the Agricultural College of Santa Catalina near Buenos Ayres, has noted the remarkable fact that the horses of the Pampas have only five. Following up his researches, he has found that the only other breed of horses in which a similar peculiarity is to be found is that of Barbary.

Taking into consideration the extreme nearness of the territories of Andalusia and Barbary, and the constant communication that in Mahommedan times must have existed between them, I am of opinion that the horses of the Pampas are evidently descended from those of Barbary.

It is not within my knowledge to state whether a similar configuration is to be observed in the Cordobese horses of to-day. But this is a point very easily cleared up.

The genet, too (the progeny of the ass and horse), has the same number of vertebræ. Is it impossible that in former times the union of an African mare and a genet may have produced the race of Berber horses which were taken by the Moors to Spain, and thence to the Pampas? The genet and the mule are not characterised by the same infecundity. During the last fifty years, in the south of France, many cases have been observed of the reproductiveness of the former animal.

The following story may serve to show that the idea of a mixed race of horses and asses that were not mules has been considered by the Arabs from the remotest ages as possible.

In the Western Soudan there are three celebrated breeds of horses, according to the Emir Abd-el-Kader—the Hâymour breed, the Bou-ghareb, and the Meizque. Of these, the Hâymour breed is considered the best, and possesses many of the same qualities that are so striking in the horses of the Pampas—speed, bottom, and robustness. The Emir says that it is not uncommon for them to perform a journey of 130 kilometres in 24 hours. I myself have frequently ridden horses of the Pampas 90 miles, and on one occasion 103 miles, in the same time.

The origin of the Hâymour breed is thus related. An Arab chief was obliged to leave a wounded mare in a small oasis, where there was grass and water, but near which no tribes ever passed. About a year afterwards, happening whilst hunting to pass the oasis, he saw his mare, well, and about to foal. Having taken her to the tents, her foal proved of singular excellence, and became the mother of a famous desert stock. The Arabs, knowing that no horses ever passed there (the wild horse is unknown in these deserts), believed that the foal was the progeny of a wild ass, Hamar-el-omâkheh, and to the foal they gave the name of Hâymour, the foal of the wild ass or onagar.

Be this as it may, whether Pegasus
or an onagar was the progenitor of the
horses of the Pampas, the fact remains
that they are renowned for the rare qualities
that made the horse of Barbary famous in
the Middle Ages. Nothing more enjoy-
able on a frosty morning than to career
over the plain, hunting ostriches on a good
horse ; nothing more fascinating (at twenty-
two) than to rattle along behind a good tropilla of ten or twelve horses, following their
mare with tinkling brass bell. Then indeed,
with silver - mounted saddle and toes just
touching the heavy silver stirrups (the
Gaucho rides long and never puts his feet
home into the stirrups, for fear of sudden
fall), you bound along over the grassy seas,
and cover perhaps 100 or 120 miles a day.

It is not only necessary in La Plata to
ride well ; a man must always fall well, that
is, on his feet. Standing once watching the
always interesting spectacle of a *domador* [1]
on horseback, with bare head and red silk
handkerchief laid turbanwise round it,
struggling with a violent colt, I rashly

[1] Horse-breaker.

remarked that he rode well. 'Yes, he sits well,' was the answer; 'let us see how he falls.' Fall he did, after one or two more plunges, and his horse, a blue and white (*azulejo*) colt, on the top of him. The colt, after a struggle or two, regained its feet; the man never stirred again. His epitaph was, 'What a pity he did not know how to fall!' 'But, after all,' remarked a bystander, 'he must have died *de puro deli-cado*' (of very delicateness), so incredible did it seem that a man could have been fool enough to let a horse fall on him. The same superstitions exist amongst the Arabs and the Gauchos as to horses and their colours. Thus, the horse with a white fore and white hind foot is sure to be fast. The Gauchos say he is crossed, *cruzado*, and that accounts for it. In the same way the Arabs say he is sure to be lucky. Both peoples unite in praising the dark chestnut. 'Alazan tostado, mas bien muerto que cansado,' says the proverb. The Arabs have a similar one. Both unite in distrust-ing a light chestnut with a white tail and mane. 'He is for Jews,' say the Arabs.

The Gauchos also assign him to an unlucky caste. 'Caballo ruano para las putas.' A dun horse, unless he have a black tail and mane and red eyes, can never be good. Only a madman would ride a horse of any colour that had a white ring round its fetlock. It is unlucky. In peace it will stumble, in war fail you. Greys will not stand the sun. The roan is slow. One striking difference though. The Arab dislikes the piebald. 'He is own brother to the cow.' The Gaucho esteems him highly. The object in life of a rich Gaucho is to have a tropilla of piebalds. The author of 'El Fausto,' a well-known Gaucho poem, makes his hero ride a piebald.

Like the Arab, the Gaucho uses long reins open at the end, to hold a horse by if he is thrown. Like the Arab, he rides upright in the saddle. Like him, too, he stands at the horse's head to mount, looking towards its tail, and catching the saddle by the pommel, instead of the cantel, like Europeans and Australians, and throws himself at one motion into the saddle without pausing in the stirrup, his horse in the

meantime going on, for no one has his
horse held in the Pampas from one end
of the 900 miles of territory from Buenos
Ayres to the Andes.   From the frontier
of Bolivia to Patagonia you will never find
a man with the heavy hands so common in
Europe.   This I attribute partly to the
severe bit and partly to the fashion of never
passing the reins through the fingers, but
holding them in the hollow of the hand,
which is carried rather high with the elbow
turned down, and not at right angles to
the body, as with us.   The Arab habit of
mounting on the off side has been dropped
by the Gaucho, but it is practised both by
the Indians of the Pampas and those of the
prairies of North America.   I had once to
mount an Indian's horse.   It proved un-
manageable till the owner called out in bad
Spanish, ' Christian frightening horse, he
mount quiet on Indian side.'   In the
Pampas he who is not an Indian is a
Christian.

Any details, even as incomplete and
rambling as are these, about the Gauchos
and their horses will soon be valuable.   This

race of tender-hearted, hospitable, nomad
creatures is passing away. I shall regret
them. I shall remember the Gaucho sailing over the Pampas, his eye fixed apparently
on nothing, yet seeing everything. I shall
remember him in his quaint costume at
the great cattle brandings, see him catch
the ostrich with the bolas, and never forget
him in his most characteristic action, viz.
when twenty-eight or thirty of them, proceeding to their respective horses, seem like
drops of water to have incorporated themselves with the horses, without noise and
without effort, and then, without the clatter
that characterises all European equestrian
performers, take wing as it were a flight of
swallows. Often during the babble of the
House of Commons, when in the hot
summer nights we are hard at work sub-
stituting the word 'and' for the word
'but,' and leaving out all the words from
'whereinsoever' down to 'which in so after'
in some senseless Bill, I shall think with
regret of the seven wild horses and the
stubborn mules which I have so frequently
seen harnessed to a diligence.

The strange, wild customs, soon to be forgotten ; the old-world life, so soon to fade away. Impressed as lines upon a picture in my memory remain the Gaucho wakes, in which the company, to light of tallow dips and the music of a cracked guitar, through the long summer nights danced round the body of some child to celebrate his entry into Paradise.

The races at the Pulperia, the fights with the long-bladed knives for honour and a quart of wine, the long-drawn melancholy songs of the Payadores, the Gaucho improvisatores, ending in a prolonged Ay—celebrating the deeds and prowess of some hero of the Independence wars—these things, these ways will disappear. Gaucho and horse, Indian with feathered lance, will go, and hideous civilisation will replace them both. In their place will rise the frightful wooden house, the drinking-house, the chapel, the manufactory. Those who are pleased with ugliness will be contented. Those who, like myself, see all too much of it already, may regret that light and colour, freedom and picturesqueness, are so rapidly being extirpated from every corner of the world.

At least we may be allowed to express the hope that in the heaven the Gaucho goes to, his horse may not be separated from him.

R. B. C. G.

IX

A VANISHING RACE

A MELANCHOLY interest attaches to anything about to go for ever. Especially
so to a people who with their customs,
superstitions, and mode of life, are doomed.
So with the Gauchos of the Pampa. Pampa,
in the Quichua tongue, signifies the 'Space.'
In truth the Pampa gives a good idea of
space. Perhaps the loneliness, the immensity
of it, has given the melancholy tinge to the
Gauchos, which is their chief characteristic.
Civilised enough to have (sometimes) a
picture of a saint in his house, to cross
himself if he hears a sudden noise at night,
still savage enough to know by the foot-
print if the horse that passed an hour ago
was mounted or running loose. A strange
compound of Indian and Spaniard, of

ferocity and childishness, a link between
ourselves and the past. A Centaur never
to be seen on foot, apt at a bargain, yet
careless of money, an inveterate smoker,
long-sighted, a poet withal, a singer and im-
proviser of melancholy wild songs. Clearly
for such a type civilisation reserves no
place. He must go. Already, I am told,
he is hardly to be met with, except on the
frontiers, and in the upper provinces of
Catamarca, Corrientes, and Santiago del
Estero.

THE RACE TWENTY YEARS AGO

I knew him but twenty years ago a force,
a maker and unmaker of presidents, a stirrer
up of revolutions, a very turbulent fellow.
He and his horse—the untiring, angular,
long-maned, fiery-eyed horse of the American
desert—must be replaced by the heavy-
footed Basque, the commonplace Canary
Islander, and the Italian in his greasy
velveteen suit. As the Gaucho replaced
the Indian, the European colonist will replace him, one more type will have faded
from the world, one more step will have

been made to universal ugliness. It becomes important therefore to preserve, however imperfectly, any characteristics, any customs that to the next generation will seem strange and incomprehensible as those of the heroes of the Niebelungen Lied. In that generation the 'Gaucho haragan,' the wandering Gaucho, with his lean horse and rusty spurs, never settled, always wandering, restless-eyed, will have disappeared, perhaps has done so already.

A CHARACTERISTIC INCIDENT

He would ride up to your house, ask for a glass of water, without dismounting pass a leg over his horse's neck, and sit talking ; perhaps make a cigarette the while, chopping the tobacco from a lump with a knife a foot long, holding his cigarette paper between his bare toes till the tobacco was fine enough cut, cursing his horse if it moved, yet annoyed if it stood still, his glance fixed on nothing apparently, yet conveying to you somehow that it took in everything of value. 'Did he want work ?' 'No, Señor.' 'Was he going

anywhere?'   'Nowhere in particular.'
'Where would he sleep?'   'Where the
night caught him.'   'Had he no arms
except that knife (*facon*)?'   'No, Señor.
God is not a bad man.'   I can see him
ride off, carrying a piece of meat tied to
his saddle, his horse cantering like a wolf.
I can see his torn poncho fluttering in the
air, hear the rattle of his iron spurs, catch
the gleam of sun falling on the handle of
his knife stuck through his sash, and sticking out on both sides like the lateen of a
Levantine boat, and reflect that usually the
morning after his visit a good horse had
disappeared, or a fat cow would be found
dead—killed for his supper.

Let him go with God, if go he must.

His long hide reins, his broken saddle
(*recado*), covered with a dirty sheepskin,
his ragged black hair, tied up in a red
handkerchief, the two bags of maté and
sugar tied to his belt, the tin kettle hanging
from his horse's headstall, his brown bare
legs shoved into top-boots (the skin of a
horse's leg, the hock forming the heel), and
his general look of contented villainy, will

not fade easily from my memory. How he lived no one knew. Where he slept only the thickest woods and most desolate water-courses could tell you.

Present at every race ; though a fine horseman, always riding a broken-down horse ; at Bahia Blanca one month, and on the frontiers of Paraguay the next ; feared by all, yet welcome for the news he brought, the Gaucho haragan was indeed a type of a past order of things.

THE TRACKER

The *rastreador*, the tracker who looked for strayed animals, found thieves, and per-formed feats that Europeans would look on as impossible, is, I suppose, also going or gone. Generally he was a little taciturn Arribeño from the upper provinces. He would arrive when horses had been stolen, dismount, seat himself by the fire, smoke a cigarette, get up, and walk out, peering at the ground, and say, without apparently looking, 'Your horses were driven off about three this morning. Two men took them, they went to the southward, one of them riding a lame horse.' 'A lame horse?' 'Yes, look at this sandy place, the horse did not put his off fore-foot down firmly.' You wondered, thinking it was chance, but saddled your horse, and followed your men, the *rastreador* every now and then pointing apparently to nothing, and saying, 'They changed horses here. Look where a saddle has been laid on the ground,' or something of the sort. Eventually he generally brought you to where the horses were, or the trail was lost in a town ; for nothing but riding through a town ever threw the human bloodhound off the track. Sometimes even then he would take up the track on the outskirts, and start off afresh. Indeed, sometimes he has been known to lead the search for stolen goods to the house of the chief magistrate of some little town, point at it and say, 'Your things are there.' This generally ended the day's sport, as Justice was, of course, blind and deaf in such cases (as in most others).

WITHOUT HORSES

'Why do you not work?' said Darwin to the Gaucho. 'I cannot, I am too poor,' was the answer. Astonishment of the great naturalist. However, the answer was most obvious to all who knew the Gaucho. The man had no horses. God had left him on foot. A Gaucho never worked except on horseback. On horseback, no matter if seventy years of age, he always appeared young. On foot he waddled like an alligator. Whether herding sheep or cattle, marching, hunting, drawing water from a well, the Gaucho always worked on horseback. He even drew a net on horseback; or churned butter by galloping about with a hide bag of milk tied to the end of a lazo. He lived on horseback, climbing when a child on to the back of an old horse, putting his little bare toes on the animal's knee and scrambling like a monkey to his seat. On the march he slept on horseback, never falling off. Coming from the Pulperia (camp stores), drunk, but quite the gentleman, he swayed backwards and forwards but kept his seat. In death, too, not seldom has a horse been found straying about with his rider, the hand that guided dead, but the sinewy legs maintaining the wild horseman seated in the saddle as in life.

THE GREATEST MISERY

The beggars, what few of them existed, begged on horseback, extending a silent hand as you passed by them. In an alarm at night every one ran to his horse, and, mounting, was ready for what might betide. We thought a horse or Gaucho was but half complete separated from each other. To be on foot was his idea of the greatest misery. A paternal Government sentenced murderers, horse thieves, and other miscreants, not to death—why rob the Republic of a man?—but to serve so many years with infantry. Miserable enough that infantry sometimes was, and those who served in it comparable as to fortune with the Christian captives who, in the Middle Ages, rowed in Turkish galleys.

The poorest man usually had at least

one tropilla of horses and a hundred mares.

MARKING HORSES

Every horse was branded with the mark of his owner—a hat, a spur, a letter, a device. The marks were the books of the Gauchos. On summer evenings they sat talking and 'painting marks' (*pintando marcas*) in the dust. 'Si Señor,' I once saw this mark on a horse ten years ago in Entre Rios. If you came upon a group of Gauchos talking, ten to one it was about horses' marks. The subject was ever new, as different marks were taken out nearly every day. When a horse was sold the owner put his mark on him twice. Thus, if the horse was marked B, the addition of another B rendered the horse unmarked— *orejano*, as it was called. The seller placed his mark on him, and he became his property. Good horses were frequently found with six or eight marks upon them. The lazo and the bolas were the tools the Gaucho worked with. With the lazo he caught horses or cattle, then threw them

down and killed or branded them. With
the bolas he caught wild or runaway horses,
and ostriches or deer. To go upon the
boleada — that is, to go out to catch
ostriches with the bolas—was the great
sport of rich and poor.

AN OSTRICH HUNT

The twilight ride to the hunting places
(many a time have I ridden it in agony of
fear on a half-wild horse) resembled a procession of shadows, the light going, unshod
horses hardly brushing the dew from the
grass, the greyhounds led carefully for fear
of startling the game. Arrived at the
places where ostriches had been seen the day
before, the company spread out in the shape
of fans, striving to encircle the birds. Then
a rush forward at full speed was made, and
the bolas commenced to whistle through
the air. Sometimes an old ostrich or two
would dash through the line, and be madly
pursued by an eager horseman twisting
the bolas round his hand, his horse rushing
like a deer, himself sitting like a statue of

bronze upon his horse. Sometimes a horseman, rushing downhill, turned a complete
somersault with his horse, but never failed
to come off on his feet, his great iron or
silver spurs clashing on the ground like
fetters. It wanted a good horse, a bold
rider, and a strong arm to make a successful
ostrich baller. But good horses, strong
arms, and bold riders were plentiful on the
Pampas in those days.

THE PAMPA INDIANS

All the Gaucho's life, though, was not
ostrich-hunting. He had the grim reality
of the Pampa Indians ever close to him.
The wild Indians (*Indios bravos*) for three
hundred years kept the frontiers in a turmoil.
Compounded as the Gaucho was of Indian
and Spaniard, still the hatred between him
and his wilder cousin the Indian was keen, as
if they had been both Christians of different
but nearly approaching sects. To the
Gaucho's heaven no Indian went. On the
plains around the mythic city of Trapalanda
no Gaucho rode.

Like the Arabs of to-day, the Indians

chiefly came to steal the Gauchos' women and horses.

In the mysterious country known as *Tierra adentro* (the inside country) quite a colony of so-called Christians lived. These Christians, chiefly unattached to any especial form of Christianity, were as a general rule Gauchos who had committed crimes and fled to the Indians for protection. Sometimes, however, after the *pronunciamiento*, which followed usually upon an election for the presidentship, some leader of the opposition had to cross the mysterious shifting line known as the frontier and sojourn for a while amongst the Indians. If so, he generally became a sort of minor chief, a *caciquillo*, as the phrase was, and took to himself a wife or two, or even three, and amongst them generally a Christian captive. About forty years ago an officer called Saá, forced, from some cause or other, to make his habitation with the Indians, rose to such eminence as almost to imperil the republic.

Don José Hernandez, the Gaucho poet, relates the adventures of one Martin Fierro,

who suffered many things with the Pampas
and Ranqueles. In the long evenings,
seated round the fire, passing the maté
round, the adventures of Martin were sure
to be discussed. The Gauchos seemed to
take him as an embodiment of themselves
and all their troubles (surely the greatest
test a poet has of popularity), and talk of
him as if at any moment he might lift the
mares' hide which acted as a door and
walk into the hut. Those of the company
who could read (not the majority) were
wont to read aloud to the unlettered from
a well-worn greasy book, printed on flimsy
paper in thin and broken type, after ex-
tracting the precious books from the recesses
of their saddle-bags, or from their riding-
boots. The others got it by heart and
then repeated it as a sort of litany.

Almost all the founders of the Argentine
Republic were of the Gaucho class. Rosas,
the tyrant of Buenos Ayres, who died a
quiet and respected country gentleman
close to Southampton, had passed his youth
on the great cattle farms (*estancias*). It is
said he could take his saddle into the

several pieces of which the *recado* (the saddle of the Pampas) is composed, and place it piece by piece upon the ground whilst galloping, and then replace it without dismounting from his horse. It is certain that in his youth he often performed the well-known Gaucho feat of jumping on a bare-backed, unbroken horse, and forcing it to obey him by sheer strength. This feat, which seems so impossible in Europe, I have often seen attempted, and sometimes executed. Urquiza, the great rival of Rosas, also was originally a country man, and so of Quiroga (the Tiger of the Llanos), Artigas, and many others. Take them for all in all, perhaps no other country ever has produced a similar class of men. The Tartars of the Steppes have been since the commencement of history banded in tribes ; so of the Arabs, Cossacks, Berbers, and Indians both of the Pampas and the Prairies of the North. The Gaucho, on the contrary, has lived a solitary life since he first came into existence as a class. In a thatched hut upon a plain as boundless as the sea without a tree, without a landmark, used to be his home. There, with his wife and children and his animals, he lived ; his nearest neighbour perhaps a league away. He hardly ever had a gun, or, if he had one, seldom ammunition, his arms being the bolas, which he jocularly called 'Las tres Marias,' a sword-blade, broken to convenient length and made a knife of, and the lazo. With this equipment he passed his life, living on meat and maté (Paraguayan tea), without a drop of milk in the midst of herds of cattle, without a vegetable, without a luxury except tobacco and an occasional glass of caña. So he became a kind of link between the Indian and the white man, a better rider than the latter, even more savagely careless of his own and others' life than the Indian of the Pampa. Not of a jealous temperament, leaving his wife and family for months, sometimes for years, and on returning not objecting to a new child or two about his hearth. Children of course are useful in the Pampas, where boys climb up the legs of a horse and ride at five years old.

A patriot too, hating all Europeans

(Spaniards especially), and despising them for their poor riding, and, like most patriots, easily befooled by knaves and made to leave his home and scour the country to restore the liberties of the republic which had never been in danger. Though quarrelsome, seldom apparently excited, but when aroused ready to kill a man with as much indifference as a bullock. Azara relates that one of them, having a quarrel with another, got off his horse and said, ' I now intend to kill you,' and taking out his knife instantly did so, the other not resisting. So it is said a Gaucho, seeing his brother groaning with rheumatic fever, unsheathed his knife and took him by the beard and cut his throat to ease his misery. Patient of hardship and starvation the Gaucho was, beyond belief. As he would say himself, it is incredible what the male Christian (*Cristiano macho*) can undergo. The race seems to have begun in the first fifty years after the Conquest ; by the middle of this century it had reached its apogee, in the time of Rosas ; when I lived amongst them they were still the dominant class in all the immense prairies of the republics of Uruguay and the Argentine Confederation. Then you might see them on a Sunday at the *pulperia*, gorgeous with silver trappings on their horses, dressed in ponchos of vicuña wool, loose black merino trousers like a Turk's, and riding-boots of patent leather stitched in patterns with red or yellow thread. Now so great has been the change you scarce can see them, and, horror of horrors, I am told that when you do, they dress in flannel shirts and trousers stuffed into their boots like Texans. Shortly, I take it, the Gaucho will wear a morning suit and buttoned boots, and play at whist instead of *truco*[1] and the *taba*.[2] When he gets off his horse he will give it to a boy to hold, instead of sitting on the *cabresto*,[3] with his knife stuck upright in the ground over his social game. It may be he and his 'china' will be married

---

[1] *Truco* was a superior kind of whist, in which the partners made signs to one another, so that the call for trump was rendered unnecessary.

[2] The *taba* was a most exciting game played with a knuckle-bone.

[3] *Cabresto* is a halter.

in a church, and that the intrusion of a little fair-haired 'Inglesito' in his family will be a thing not to be tolerated. Polo will take the place of barebacked races on the *caucha*, and when his horse at night falls into a hole the man will fall upon his head instead of on his feet. Before that time I hope in Buenos Ayres some sculptor of repute will do a statue of a Gaucho and his horse, for since the riders in the Parthenon no horseman has been at once so strong and picturesque upon his horse.

Bolas, lazo, Gaucho, Indian all will soon have gone, if to Trapalanda I know not, but I hope so. Men will rob in counting-house and on exchange with pen and book, instead of on the highway with *trabuco* and *facon*. The country is getting settled, I have little doubt ; cheap Spanish Bibles will soon be forced on those who cannot read them ; the long-horned Spanish cattle will be replaced by Hereford or shorthorn ; where the ostrich scudded the goods train will snort and puff. Happy those who like the change, for they will have their way. Civilisation, which more surely plants its empty sardine tin as a mark on the earth's face than ever Providence placed its cross (on purpose to convert Constantine) in the sky, and the hideous pall of gloom and hypocrisy which generally accompanies it, will have descended on the Pampas. Instead of the quaint announcements of strayed horses, signed by the Alcalde, on the *pulperia* door, a smug telegraph clerk at the wooden wayside station will inform the delighted inhabitants of the continued firmness of grey shirtings. *Ay de mi !* Pampa !

R. B. C. G.

X

YUSTE

THE muleteer, answering some unexpressed questioning of my eyes, says, 'Yes, that is Yuste.' For more than an hour the bridle-path has twisted and turned in serpentine convolutions, under the shadow of deep chestnut forests, and we have come out on to a vast country, rolling into hills and valleys until it is met by the great wooded mountains profiled against the vivid midday sky. In the midst of this immensity of mountain and forest and sky, high up on the mountain side, a speck amidst the billowy undulations of the forests in which it is almost buried, a white building glitters in the sun. It can only be some decaying and desolate monastery nestling amidst solitudes so austere and unpeopled—'the grim and horrid' deserts of the monastic chroniclers of the seventeenth century, already alien to the spirit which took men to the wastes and mountains, already oblivious of the charm which these sweet and savage spots exercised on the simple and enthusiastic contemplative of a bygone generation.

Presently we begin to descend the heights which command this great unbroken landscape—these green distances, which convey an undefinable and vague expression of eternity, of a something that never ends. It is now too steep to ride—the path too rough, too narrow. The sun is burning, and the cistus, the heather, and the furze—the only and universal vegetation which covers the burnt and sandy soil—fill the air with strange and arid perfumes.

A river, agitated, bubbling, merry, rushes through the bottom of the valley, sending a thousand rhythmical cadences through the hot silence—a silence that is almost oppressive. We cross its mediæval bridge, too narrow except for mule and

man. It is midday as the mules splash
through the watercourses which form the
streets of Cuacos—Cuacos, whence the
little rascals of the sixteenth century stole
the Emperor's favourite cherries ; Cuacos,
with its brown, unwhitewashed houses,
which conserve all the dim mystery of
their antiquity, their wooden balconies
mouldering slowly to dust in the sun.
On either side of the all but intransitable
street the impenetrable shadow of arched
doorways form dark spots, which cut
trenchantly on the glaring sunlight. We
are in full mediævalism. Time has stood
still, and we are in a town of the time of
Philip II.

Mediæval the wine-shop, open to the
street, before which our mules stop in-
stinctively. Mediæval the dark-green
bottles, shaped like an alchymist's alembics,
in which the swarthy, merry-faced *posadera*
(innkeeper) hands us wine. Mediæval
her costume, the bundle of gay-coloured
petticoats which she sways with that undefinable movement of the hips peculiar
to the Spaniard ; her hair, braided in a

fashion that one may still see in Velasquez's
pictures, combed into great glossy wheels
which curl in front of each ear, from which
dangle rough earrings of massive silver ;
silver rings gleam on her supple, brown
hands, a silver necklace round her throat.
Presently the whole town surrounds us,
but she is still the spokeswoman. Curious
questioning, merry answering, sly jesting
with my handsome young muleteer ; but
it is neither prudent nor safe to linger too
long in a Spanish village, lost to the world
in the depths of Estremadura, and, followed
by the curious gaze of man, woman, and
child, we take our way to Yuste.

We have ridden, perhaps, half an hour
under a burning sun. We are ascending
always — a slow, almost imperceptible,
ascent up the side of the mountain, which
a few hours ago, as we looked at it from
the shadow of the chestnut-woods, seemed
so far away. A grey wall, into which is
built the sculptured arms of Austria, peers
through the leaves of the oak-forest. A
moment more, and we enter the great
convent gates of Yuste, where, centuries

ago, a prior, moved by intensest emotion, welcomed a wearied and disillusioned man, who was nevertheless the greatest monarch of Europe and of his age.

A courtyard, green, mouldering, sunlit, invaded by the gigantic shadow of the historic walnut-tree under which Charles loved to sit, and which even then was accounted a patriarch of the forest—a courtyard moss-grown, strewn with withered leaves, its corners full of damp and vague dimness ; a fountain decaying slowly in the centre, from which the water trickles feebly into a great granite basin choked with leaves and rubbish. My muleteer stares somewhat vacantly around him. Is it for this, then—to see an old ruined building, full of sadness and decay—that a sane person braves the chilliness of dawn, the broiling heat of the midday sun, to take a long and comfortless journey, with its accompanying hunger and fatigue? The shadow of the walnut-tree has crept on and on through the centuries, until it has gained the granite mounting-block on the other side of the court. There for the last time the 'prince of light horsemen' mounted feebly his old blind pony. There, too, I insist on getting down.

In front of us stands the 'palace'—for so it has remained, and will remain for ever, in the mouths of these simple country people—a modest building two storeys high, the upper one opening on to a balcony supported by wooden pillars, exposed to the full blaze of the sun. It is reached by a vaulted causeway, the incline of which is almost imperceptible. In a moment we are standing on the very spot in the corridor whence on a bright placid day in early autumn Charles watched for the last time the afternoon sun shining over the great walnut-tree full into the gallery. It was here that he felt the premonitory pangs of his fatal illness, and gazed for the last time on the sunlit Vera. The key grates in the lock, and we are suddenly invaded by a sense of shadow and gloom. And yet these small, low-roofed rooms, which differ but little from monastic cells, still full of the strange atmosphere of the past, witnessed the

closing scenes of a life and a career than
which none has ever been more brilliant,
and for which Europe itself was all too
small a stage. Transverse beams of heavy
chestnut-wood, cut in the neighbouring
forests, cross each other overhead. Time
has tinged them with a darker hue, and
generations of spiders have spun their webs
unchallenged in the deep recesses of their
angles. Narrow casements pierced in the
profound thickness of the massive walls
admit the light, but a light already attenu-
ated by the deep shadow of the roofed
balcony without. The inner rooms are
dimmer still. That one dimmest of all
where, centuries ago, the gentle William
van Male, watching the royal deathbed,
whispered breathlessly to the Archbishop
of Toledo, standing in the shadow of the
doorway, *Domine, jam moritur*—'My lord,
he is now dying.' The mystery of that
death—that last scene of agony and
struggle—still envelops it.

The wooden shutters are thrown back,
and the hot sun streams into what was
once the Emperor's cabinet. Heaving a

sigh of relief, we step out into the balcony
and lean over the roughly-carved balustrade
which overhangs the terraced garden. If
any scene can dispel the melancholy con-
jured up by these faded reminiscences, it
is that which lies stretched before us in
the dreamy stillness of the afternoon. A
tangled wilderness of beauty sleeps beneath
us in the sun. The grey walls and wooden
balconies, the glossy orange-trees, the roses
which trail over the little path which skirts
its brim, are reflected vaguely, dimly, in
the motionless depths of the fish-pond
embowered amidst the interlacing foliage
of mulberry and orange trees. Here and
there a thick curtain of green slime, which
seems the slow and undisturbed deposit
of centuries, blots out the images which
lie in its slumbrous depths. The low walls
which surround it, grey with the greyness
of the ages, are crumbling gently to decay
——but a decay how graceful, how sweet
and gentle! Tufts of wild mint grow out
of the interstices of the stonework, and
kiss their own reflection in the placid
water. And over all is the sun, and all

is unchanged. Time has stood still for Yuste, and only the forms are wanting which have flitted through it and rotted to dust—the footfall of a royal solitary, the vague hum of life, the sound of voices.

'And here lived,' says my muleteer musingly, dimly comprehending, 'a king —he whom they say was Emperor' (Mikado would have conveyed as much to him); 'and this is El Palacio!'

The sunlight is once more blotted out, and we are standing in the raised choir of the church—silent, cold, and desolate— from which, not so many years ago, midnight orisons, sad monotonous *misereres*, still rolled so sadly into the vaulted nave beneath. It may be that those grey walls still retain, chained up in their stony impenetrability, the far-away reverberations of those forgotten prayers. Great choir- books lie rotting on carved stands. I open one. The dust and mildew fly out in a cloud. It shuts down with a clang which echoes through the empty church, and sends a sudden chill to the heart.

High above, in the dim recesses of the

roof to the left of the high altar—that
high altar which not half a century ago
was ablaze with ornament and gilded
sculpture ; before which silver lamps swung
before the Host, and monks passed up and
down the tall steps before it, their habits
scarcely brushing them as they passed ;
now stripped, desecrated, heartrending—
hangs the chestnut coffin in which the
monks of Yuste laid their royal benefactor
and brother—yea! death makes us all
brothers—to rest. Long did it lie beneath
the high altar, so that the priest in the
solemn act of consecration might stand
over a dead man's prostrate face—long
after the body which it contained had been
borne away from those peaceful glades, to
lie decaying in the Royal Pudridero of the
Escorial, and to afford Philip IV. the
opportunity of saying his one recorded
sentence. When the coffin was opened
and the body of his great ancestor, who
in life ruled from Wurtzburg to Acapulco,
was exposed to view, he turned to D. Luis
de Haro and remarked, 'Honrado cuerpo,
Don Luis,' receiving the formal Castilian

reply, ' Muy honrado, Señor.' Curious
visitors, possessed of the vapid irreverence
of our age, chipped bits of the strong
chestnut-wood to bear with them to those
stupid collections of bric-à-brac and bad
museums which modern man calls his
house. But it was not until a rich American offered to buy the relic and transport
it bodily to Boston that Spanish pride
caught fire, slung it up there in the shadow
of the roof, where even the long lean arm
of an American was powerless to reach it,
and so saved it from the devastating hands
and vulgar greed of the sightseer.

Little remains of that great monastery
which hid its splendour amidst the shadowy
chestnut glades and mountain fastnesses of
that wild Estremeñan desert. Like that
most gorgeous relic of the Geronomites,
the Parral of Segovia, heaps of carved stone
lying buried amongst the débris encumber
the great cloisters. Here and there a wall
stands intact, in which arched windows,
framing the sunshine, are like the vacant
orbits of a dead man's eye.

A little wind—a sough, a sigh almost

imperceptible — sweeps through the oak-trees, and the dead leaves of the year that is gone rustle slowly and gently on the path, which, through alleys of box which have long since lost all shape and form and curious culture of man's hand, leads through the oak forest to the Hermitage of Belem. Most pathetic of all is the desolation of this little ruined sanctuary — a veritable sanctuary of the forest, enclosed within the monastery bounds — the goal of the Emperor's walks.

As we turn away from the great court-yard of Yuste, and as our mules clatter sharply over the stony path, we are invaded by an immense sadness. It is as if we had buried a friend—laid to rest some phase of life never to revive.

We sleep under the shadow of those same chestnut forests whence we had caught our first glimpse of Yuste in the morning —a spot well retired from the road, which I had then mentally chosen for our camp-ing-ground that night. All night I lay in a sort of stupor. All sorts of travellers are passing on that silent road beneath !—

but, no ; it is only the sound of a mule browsing amongst the ferns and oak-scrub, or the twitch of the rope which hobbles his feet.

In the grey, vague, vaporous light of dawn the fire has burnt low, and the muleteer is bending over a heap of white ashes lighting his cigarette. It is time to saddle up. As we emerge on to the road again, as before, he turns—'Señora,' he says, and there is an inflection in his voice which it had not the first time, 'that is Yuste.'

That is Yuste—those great mountains over which the mist is sweeping, and which throws a curtain of hazy uncertainty over wood and vale and dale, in which I can distinguish nothing but a dark spot, yet so faint and ill defined that it may be only fancy. But both the muleteer and I know where that lies which we vainly seek with our eyes, and we both say together, ' Adios, Yuste ! ' And my servant adds, ' Hasta siempre ! '—' Until for ever ! '

G. C. G.

XI

THE BATUECAS

I HAVE been in the strangest, wildest, most forgotten corner of Spain, molested by the feet of few wanderers from civilisation since the Middle Ages, and those eccentrics like myself, to whom the past lives more vividly than the present ; a corner round which cluster legends half terrible, half comic, in their fantastic weirdness and strangeness. As I write in the long low whitewashed room of the rude *venta* or wayside inn —the *fondak* of the Arabs, the *meson* of Mexico ; its floor on the same level, and paved with the same rough cobble-stones, as the street outside, and the zaguan or great covered porch into which it opens from the inside, around which last night muleteers, shepherds, charcoal-burners, laid

their blankets, and slept in close proximity
to their mules and donkeys—it seems that
I have awakened from a dream. And yet
nothing can be stranger, farther away from
the regions of commerce and railways, than
those roughly-hewn massive beams of
chestnut-wood of the roof above my head,
or the thick solid plank of chestnut-wood
which serves for a door, with its leathern
latch hooking on to a nail inside.

Nothing more curious and old world
than the figures which gathered last night
around the corkwood fire in the middle of
the kitchen, seeking a night's shelter like
myself for themselves and beasts, alternately
lit up or thrown into sudden shadow by
the fiery glow of its fitful blaze — rich
labourers and farmers from the wild
mountain districts of Salamanca and Estremadura, bound to the cattle fair at Plasencia
—shepherds, goatherds, muleteers. Their
coarse embroidered shirts made by the
women at home ; loose knee-breeches with
silver buttons and gay silk tags, the last
decree of fashion in Philip's IV.'s time ;
short, bright-coloured velveteen coats and

broad sashes conserved something of the antiquity of another age, kept alive in villages and rude farmhouses, which the restless changing world has passed over as beneath its notice. Mediæval, too, our hostess stooping over and tasting the contents of her pipkins and brown dishes, stirring up the savoury mess of dried cod-fish and red peppers for our supper.

And yet to me, who am still dreaming of the fantastic fairyland between which and me lie days of weary travel, how tame, how conventional, how trite seems this scene, so quaint and picturesque! I have come from a place and scenes so dreamlike that what would at other times have been so strange to me rouses in me the faintest, most languid interest.

My muleteers have said good-bye to me in the cold light of the dawning day. What the strange reluctance?—the dollars clinked and counted and stowed away in the coarse canvas bag between the folds of their sash; what this strange reluctance to say farewell which overpowers both me and them?—me, the inhabitant of another world, in whose ears still linger the bustle of cities and the rattle of the railway train, although at heart half a sylvan ; and these wild mountaineers, who wish me God-speed in strange guttural accents—half-unintelligible accents—which conserve the trace of something noble and musical—of a race as free as the winds, as careless, as unrestrained.

The long days spent together amidst fragrant wastes, where the silence which reigned over the monotony of mountain tracks so interminable that it seemed they would never end was alone broken by the mules' hoofs, forge a bond which costs a pang to sunder. Hence this sudden irresolution, this mysterious emotion, spontaneous and instinctive, which overpowers us both.

A week ago we had never seen each other's faces. To-morrow I shall be absorbed into a world which exists only to them as a sort of fairy-like fantastic legend, and they will traverse and retraverse for many, many morrows those wild mountain paths and deserts of Estremadura, which will for me alone exist in fancy and in memory.

Within an hour I shall be rattled back again, in a ramshackle coach drawn by six mules, into the world. I shall bear away with me a recollection of long sunlit days spent in traversing flowery wastes ; of mules creeping along goat-tracks winding zigzag along mountain-sides which never seemed to end, buried amidst giant heaths and cistus, with large white blossoms blotched at the heart with a single vivid stain of red, which caught at our clothes as we passed, and impregnated them with their strange, powerful, resinous fragrance ; mountain and plain a tangled wilderness of flowery brush-wood, penetrable only to its denizens, the wolf, the wild boar, the fox. Of essences of flowers crushed under the hoofs of the mules, and a thousand aromatic scents laden with life and healing, filling the hot balsamic atmosphere, which burned and scorched our faces and hands ; of mysterious and unseen insect life, which buzzed and chirped, and filled the air with strange and drowsy murmurs. Then, the cistus left behind, of heights less clothed, more open, beneath which dashed rushing, brawl-

ing rivers, at which we dared not look for
very giddiness ; and the eye swept over
the grand wide lines of horizons flowing
one into another, until they seemed lost in
eternity — depths of plain and mountain
covered with an undulating growth of wild
arbutus, which melted away at last in a
faint haze that might have been the sea.
I remember stopping for breakfast at a
farmhouse, where scarlet peonies grew
thick amongst a patch of green corn, which
the mules snatched at as they passed, and
the hum of bees round the sunlit porch,
where we feasted on milk and goat's-milk
cheese. I remember passing through
several towns and villages which plunged
us straight into the Middle Ages (ourselves
the only anachronism)—old, stained, lichen-
covered, the streets, through the middle
of which ran streamlets and watercourses,
impassable on foot, where groups of men
in their cleanest shirts and holiday velvet-
eens and silver buttons (it was Sunday),
congregated together in the market-place,
stared at us curiously, as the smith shod
one of our mules that had cast its shoe ;

and children crowded round us in wonder and amazement, but not impertinence ; and an innkeeper—a veritable Sancho Panza— offered us wine in a Salamanca jug, and smacked his lips with glee when we told him it was good—and it was ! Of villages where from year's end to year's end the entire population lives on bread and wine, and goat's milk is an expensive luxury.

Tired, hungry, footsore, shoeless, ragged, we forget it all as we limp past the rude slate cross which marks the enchanted boundaries of the Batuecas.

We have yet a league to go, but the road made by the monks is good. On this road hundreds of friars have passed, going to and from the monastery, many to their living grave in the Batuecas. I wonder if this savage grandeur, this brown and limpid river which flows beneath the beetling crags and towering peaks, clothed with woods untouched by the hand of man since the Creation, affected them as it does me, or if they passed on, their cowl lowered over sunken and lack-lustre eye, wrapped up in a Deity which they adored in the

hidden recesses of their own mysterious
imaginings ?

Am I wandering—have I lost my head
in reading those legends of a distant age ?—
or is this strange spot, whose existence the
Middle Ages accounted a myth, under the
spell of some enchantment ? Those fantastic
forests which arrest me with such a strange,
such a weird impression of life petrified and
arrested in the midst of motion, but not
destroyed ; where the blanched ghosts of half
decaying trees dead long years ago, from
which the grey moss hangs in long ragged
shreds, fling their ghastly skeletons against
the fresh green foliage of early summer ;
those boughs which overhang the stream
and bend down to kiss it ; those trunks
and branches which seem to fight and
struggle with each other for space and
light ; that sense of life, expression, and
feeling with which the very twigs seem to
be instinct ;—exercises a strange and undefinable fascination, and suggests strange
secrets concealed within their depths.

A distant hermitage gleaming on a
height amongst the cork-trees ; a sudden

widening out of the narrow glen; a clump
of huge horse-chestnuts, brought by some
brother from the ' Indies,' looking so strange
here amidst a vegetation so different ; tall
cypresses of secular growth towering above
the bell-tower of a gateway, forming depths
of shadow impressed with I know not what
obscure melancholy, to which the murmuring
of the stream and the constant rush of its
waters lend a monotonous undertone.   It
needs not the apocalyptic figure of a saint
in the niche above to tell us that we have
arrived at the famous—the most famous in
Spain—Carmelite Desert of Batuecas.

Above the current of the waters, the
bell rung by so many pilgrims, so many
friars, so many wanderers and penitents in
years which now seem so far away, clangs
harshly on the silence, and once more the
river takes up the burden of its song.

Wooden bars fall to the ground ; a rough
figure, clad in sheepskin, greets us as in
surprise ; we enter the gate-house, where
the figures of kneeling saints in the
niches in the corners contrast strangely
with the donkey tethered there. A flagged

causeway, bordered by an avenue of lofty
cypress-trees, leads through a garden—out
of which Time has not blotted the quaint
shapes of the box-bushes, once so daintily
trimmed, nor quite banished the tangled
flowers, which fall about our feet—past a
marble fountain in which the water still falls
drearily, to the church. There is nothing of
architectural curiosity in this plain brick
church, in these rude and simple cells,
each with its inclined plank which formed
the Carmelite's bed, the invariable skull
and cross rudely carved of cork : only a
great pathetic sadness, an intense abandon-
ment. It is strange to see their little altars
which surround the cloisters almost intact,
in each a figure of some strange solitary
caged in a little grotto made of shells, in
which here and there a skull or human bone
preaches its stern sad lesson ; strange to see
the herbs still green and flowering in the
herb-garden, although it is so many years
since the hand of the Brother who doctored
the sick and ailing gathered the last leaf,
distilled the last healing essence. We
wander through the cells disconsolately,

touching the little odds and ends which the
friars left behind them in their flight : a
rude cross, left lying on a casement; the
wine jars, untouched since then, which lie
useless in the cellars ; the buildings, once
busy with the sound of adze and saw ; the
smithy, where they forged all the ironwork
they wanted for church or monastery ; the
neglected vines and olive-trees, which still
climb sparsely up the hill in the terraces of
the monks ; the corn-mill, which the water
turns no more, ready for use to-morrow ;
the oil-mill, where the jars were filled for
the use of the convent.

So lived this community, which built
all and made all for itself ; which turned a
desert into a flowering garden, adequate to
its own subsistence and simple wants ; and
when the last echoes of the sandalled feet
of the expelled friars sank into silence—just
retribution for the folly and pride of man
—it became again a wilderness, useless,
uncultivated, fit only to give pasture to a few
herds of goats.

In the gathering twilight I climb up the
hill to one of the sixteen hermitages which,

like the Laura of the Cenobites of Egypt, perched on inaccessible crags, surround and overlook the monastery below. Lost amongst the thick forest of corkwood, up heights so steep that a false step would have hurled me down into the rapid river below, after half an hour's climb I reach the disroofed hermitage. The cypress still rears itself into the evening sky; the stream still runs before the door; the cupboard is there in which the hermit stored his meal of dried fruit; the altar, with its lovely sixteenth-century tiles, waits for the footfall of the sad and solemn solitary; the bell hangs in the bell-tower, only the touch of a hand is wanted!

As night came on, and the mists shrouded the Peña de Francia[1] from our vision, from the gateway of the monastery we watched the great herds of goats driven into the corral. All the evening we had heard their bells tinkling afar off in the rocky crags. The tinkling came nearer and nearer, and at last the barking of the wolf-dogs, the cracking of the whips of the brown savage

---

[1] A high mountain which overhangs the valley.

who trudged along after them, dressed in
sheepskin, winding his horn, heralded their
approach.

An inexplicable sadness brooded over
the dusky kitchen—the kitchen of the
friars—where we sat far into the night
round the red blaze of cork logs, and goat-
bells tinkled below or a wolf-dog bayed,
and listened to the curious lore which
Nature and legend teach to the half-
inarticulate children who live closest to
her bosom. Legends as fantastic as the
blaze of the fire, which cast strange
flickerings of light into the blackness of
the patriarchal kitchen, become vivified,
and receive substance and colour in the
comments of these rustic mouths. They
look upon me with almost mysterious awe,
the same almost as that with which some
great scholar might be looked upon by the
simpler minds of the Middle Ages, as I
produce my store of cheap-Jack learning
got out of faded monkish chronicles and
handbooks.

How the Batuecas, haunt of evil spirits
and demons, shut away from all communi-

cation with the world outside, a malignant
spot shunned by the shepherds, its very
existence looked on as doubtful in the
Middle Ages, until a lovely lady of the
House of Alba, seeking shelter for her
illicit love with a page, discovered these
solitudes peopled with a wild sylvan race,
speaking an unintelligible tongue which
preserved a few words of Gothic; how by
some they were supposed to be Goths, by
others Arabs; how the appearance of a
convent in a spot so wild and savage was
looked upon with superstitious dread, as
having sprung up in a single night by some
dread miracle, and likely to disappear again
in the same strange way ; until we peopled
the solitude with the creatures of our fancy,
and heard the Carmelite habits brush
through the garden alleys, and the simul-
taneous sound of the hermitage bells borne
to us on the wind, and fancied as we looked
out of the casement into the night that we
saw lights flickering and shadowy figures
passing to and fro against the glow in the
ruined windows of the church.

On the rude bed strange visions and

fantasies disturbed my sleep. By a physical reaction I was still counting the measured tread of my mules' hoofs, which rang rhythmically through my brain, when a figure stood before me, and, growing larger and gradually more distinct, a stern Carmelite brother of gigantic stature barred my progress——, and I awoke to find the world soaked with rain.

We watched the goats milked below, and after a bowl of milk and a piece of bread—our only breakfast, our only food, indeed, throughout the whole long day—in the grey of the early morning, blotted out by the rain, the convent of the Batuecas disappeared from our sight.

G. C. G.

XII

LA VERA DE PLASENCIA

A DISTRICT which it would almost seem
that Nature herself has been at pains to
isolate from the surrounding world ; shut
in by mountain barriers ; little visited ;
innocent of roads ; the communication
between the towns and villages, difficult at
all times, ceases entirely to exist in winter.
An ocean of billowy prairie, which sweeps
away until it melts into dazzling and radi-
ant distances ; shaggy chestnut forests untouched by the woodman's axe for centuries ;
wild streams which dash down roaring and
impetuous from mountain gorges ; red-
roofed towns and villages hidden in undulations of the ground or clinging to mountain
slopes ; a brief compendium of aromatic
waste and savage precipice, of forest glade

and alpine solitude—this is the Vera ; a brief compendium indeed, for the whole district can be ridden over with ease within a week. A district over which hangs a strange halo of romance ; which is indelibly associated with perhaps the most curious and picturesque episode of Spanish history ; for a white building, which glimmers midway up a mountain side, among undulating chestnut woods, is for ever haunted by the gigantic figure of a disillusioned man, who held the strings on which all Europe danced like puppets—is the Geronomite Monastery of Yuste.

Nor it alone, for it would seem that it hovers persistently over the immense solitude and tranquil loneliness of the entire Vera. He who has so long rotted to dust in the oblivion of the melancholy chamber of the Escorial, still lives in the memories of these rude villagers, whose unruly ancestors stole his cherries before they, too, faded from time and the memory of their kind. To hear them talk, it might have been yesterday that the great Emperor took up his abode among their midst ; but

yesterday that the funeral dirges rolled
through the monastery church of Yuste.
From Yuste it is only a summer afternoon's
ride over a wide mountain pass to Jarandilla,
where, in the feudal castle of the Counts of
Oropesa, he lodged.   Above Jarandilla,
among the peaks of the snow-capped
mountains, is the pass still known as the
Emperor's, whence Charles for the first
time saw rolled out before him in autumnal
beauty the vast expanse of the Vera, and
which he affirmed with truth would be his
last.   Strange that this wild nook of in-
comparable beauty, lost amid the burning
deserts of Spain, should have haunted
his memory on the hot battle-field of
Germany ; should have become for him, the
active, fiery soldier, the consummate and
crooked diplomatist, his desired haven of
rest.

NIGHT IN THE OLD TOWNS

Nothing more picturesque than to reach
one of the towns at nightfall after a long
day on horseback.   A light twinkling from
an iron cresset points out the Posada, and

the traveller is swallowed up in the shadow of its doorway. Round a corkwood fire, which blazes in the middle of the floor, the smoke going out through the rafters of the roof, sits a heterogeneous collection of travellers—muleteers, a wool merchant from Salamanca, a pedlar, a priest bound to a distant village. The hostess squats over the fire, preparing the supper in red pipkins, now and then taking part in the conversation, flinging back a sharp sarcasm in answer to the jokes of the assembly. We leave the Posada at break of day. In the plaza the smith is already at work, shoeing mules and donkeys, surrounded by a crowd of labourers. The women, their heads covered with their petticoats, for the air is sharp, chatter and scream and gesticulate around the fountain, above which tower the grey walls of the church. A lane, inundated at every step by cascades of water, winds down between banks and moss-grown walls, hung over with gnarled walnut trees and cherry blossom, to the ivied bridge we crossed last night. On a beetling crag which overhangs the seething stream is perched a little hermitage embowered in foliage. The entrances of all the villages in the Vera are thus guarded and sanctified.

All is silent except for the church bells, which still echo lugubriously on the stillness of the atmosphere, as if they centred all of life and motion in the ghostly town. Jarandilla, the most important of the towns of the Vera, once the residence of the Counts of Oropesa, a branch of the great house of Alba, in whose castle Charles was lodged pending his translation to Yuste, is abandoned to a few villagers, who cultivate the surrounding soil, and whose life, when all else around them has crumbled to dust, by a strange turn of fate remains virtually the same now as then. They are proud of the grim old castle, which gives such an imposing air of nobility to their conglomerations of picturesque huts. They ask as they point out the massive turrets and gates, which seem as if they would defy all time, and the musicians' gallery with its geometrical parapet of stone, which still faces the grass-grown courtyard, once the scene of many a tilting at the ring, and

Moorish cane play and bull-fight, whether in 'those worlds over there,' pointing to a vague spot on the horizon, 'there can be such a monument as this.' 'Confess,' they say jealously, 'that you have never seen anything like it before.' I am fain to say I never have. The coloured tiles still cling to the mouldering walls. The rafters of the roof still cross each other overhead, whole and entire. In a garden of the neighbouring monastery, where, among the pleasant shade of orange and fig trees, the Emperor wiled away the sunniest hours of a December day, a fountain still bears his name.

THE VERA DOOMED

I have ridden through the Vera in early spring, when its villages are buried in white blossom ; in the hot summer, when the air is full of scents of wild thyme and sage and rosemary ; in October, when the first faint sigh whispers through the boughs of its great chestnut forests, and the leaves flutter down slowly on to the path beneath. I have slept under its clear starlight nights—

the midday halts beside a pure stream or
on the edge of a forest are still present before me. I see the great prairie rolling
away to the sky—vague, undefined, sug-
gesting infinite space, flecked with cattle or
flocks of sheep, while some herdsman, a
wild and imposing figure, breaks the
monotony of the horizon. Its loveliness
and loneliness affect me strangely. I may
perhaps, however, be the last to see it as it
exists to-day, with its patriarchal rural life,
its antiquated and picturesque mode of
agriculture, its strange atmosphere of mediævalism, for the last time I was at Yuste I
heard an ominous whisper that it was to be
purchased by a rich capitalist, who was
about to make a carriage road and gradually
open up the district. If so, the loveliest,
the strangest, the wildest district of Spain
is doomed to destruction. The discontent
with existing conditions will make itself felt.
The people will exchange the very solid
and real happiness they now enjoy, together
with their freedom, for an illusory phantom
in the air. The sons will barter the lands of
their fathers to flock into the neighbouring

town to become the prey of the capitalist, while the latter, patting his stomach with self-conscious virtue, points out to a melancholy plain, intersected by enclosures, shorn of its forests and the aromatic growth which covered its interminable prairies, and which is all that remains of the lovely Vera as Charles V. saw it, and as it may still be seen to-day. Nay, more, we may even hope that civilisation may make such rapid strides that a Bible pedlar shall yet be seen at the entrance of the Great Geronomite Monastery, speaking to the people in an unknown tongue, or a strange dialect purporting to be Spanish ; while in the courtyard, where the Prince of Light Horsemen mounted for the last time his old white one-eyed pony, a red cigarette machine ' functions,' bearing the inspiriting inscription of ' pennies only.'

G. C. G.

XIII

IN A GARDEN

I FANCY that at the beginning of this century soldiers were not much given to analysing motives. They fought, marched, counter-marched, killed, and were killed, without inquiring why or caring wherefore. I am aware that their behaviour was *du dernier bourgeois*, but I do not care in the least. Not that war—its pomps, military bands, forage caps, wounds, ulcers, hospitals, and national neglect of the survivors—delights me much, or at all. No ; would that soldiers were only to be seen stuffed, or preserved in spirits in museums. Save only, of course, the Life Guards, who should survive if but on account of their helmets and their black horses. Still, a soldier who ' done his level best,' through snow, through heat, in hunger, and in thirst, despite the follies of the War Office, and who at last rests in a garden overlooking his last stricken field, appeals to me somehow, if only for the garden's sake. Such a garden too !—shaded by acacias, girt by grey walls grown over with valerian and with umbelliferæ, on a peninsula jutting out to sea. *In prælio occisus*, etc., the Latin has it. The English : ' To the memory of General Sir John Moore, killed at Elviña, near Coruña, while covering the embarkation of the British troops.' Somehow, I like *In prælio occisus* better than ' killed in action ' ; it sounds more martial.

Coruña, the Groyne of the Elizabethans, a busy little place with trade in oxen and in onions, tobacco factory (La Palloza), like a scene in *Carmen*, its three fiords of El Ferrol, Betanzos, and la ria de Coruña ; with its barelegged fisher-girls, its ox carts in the streets, its churches, houses with balconies enclosed with glass, and Plaza de Maria Pita, is known, I fancy, best in England by its association with him who lies in the Jardin de San

Carlos, *In prælio occisus.* If not it should
be so. Let them cremate who will, bury in
vaults, in churches, under alabaster, with
due (unfaithful) epitaph, I still hold that
in the sea or near the sea a man rests best.
Not that I love the sea, with memories of
stewards, smell of oil, and stuffy cabins.
Far from it!

Yet the sound of waves should (nay
does, I am sure) sound pleasant to ears
that have heard much noise in life of
cannon, rattling cabs, or prattling fools.
Besides, the vegetation by the sea grows
sparsely, as if it were not nourished by
what lies under it, the only thing repulsive
in your country churchyard, though even
that is mitigated when one sees the par-
son's pony feeding among the tombstones.
Therefore, when the question comes to
local option I shall vote for cemeteries by
the sea. Along the narrow streets is the
Church of Santiago, Romanesque in style,
with low round doors, the arch supported
on bullocks' heads of stone, with the fattest
lamb I ever saw in stone in the middle
of the arch; above St. James himself, on a

somewhat long-backed horse, trampling
upon the Moorish dogs like a true Christian.
Within, a fledgling priest essaying his first
Latin sermon, with much of ' Autem mei
filii ; dixit Sanctus Ambrosius,' to a congregation chiefly composed of brother
priests, apparently assembled like actors at
a *matinée* to ' give a hand.'

Leaving the church, the assembled
priests, the fishermen, the villagers, and
the perspiring neophyte in the pulpit, across
the Plaza de la Constitucion, passing the
Audiencia, at last one reaches a curious,
fort-like structure, circular in form, with
the embrasures all glazed like windows,
God knows why ; and the usual Spanish
gateway, built for all time, with the arms
of Castile and Leon sculptured upon it,
with two tall, shady elms on either side the
entrance. Inside, a sort of half Italian
garden cut in squares by myrtle hedges,
and with tall bushes of purple veronica and
escalonia, Italian as to form, but Spanish,
purely Spanish, in neglect. Gardens, I
fancy, should be wild in spite of Verulam ;
even a weed or two (that is a Southern

weed) lends grace to the formal garden
plants. It is as if a gipsy (from the Bohemia
of our dreams) had strayed into a ball-
room. In the middle, the grave ; like
most graves, leaving something to be
desired in taste, still not unpleasing, with
its plain sarcophagus of granite, supported
on a massive slab of stone. It had been
better had not the Municipality, in its zeal
and kindliness, painted the stone in buff
and grey to the glory of God and England.
About the square acacias stand sentinel, at
the four corners clumps of pampas grass.
It always seems to me that pampas grass
looks sad in Europe, and hangs its head as
if it missed wild horses bounding over it,
and sickened for the calling of the Teru-
tero.

It may be, too, that want of water in
this case was the cause, for your Spanish
gardener, I should fancy, watered but fit-
fully, except, perhaps, in winter. Be this
as it may, if pampas grass does not mourn
itself, it makes me sad, as when I see a
branded horse from the pampas in a London
cab. Surely to the horse at least remem-

brances must come in the fetid streets of his *querencia*, of the free life, fresh grass, the little foals he played with, and the wild gallops under some Gaucho wilder than himself; for have not 'learned clerkes' assured us that animals do think, though, if they do, I am glad they cannot write their impressions of mankind? So round the grave grow pampas grass, veronica, myrtle, escalonia, datura, golden rod, and fennel, and many another flower the General trod upon in life and may be never saw, being occupied with things as transitory and quite as unimportant.

Let him sleep on in the little garden by the sea, close to the barracks where the Spanish soldiers cry, 'Alerta centinela!' Perhaps the sound of arms and drums and barrack life would please him better, could he hear them, than the swishing of the sea.

They say that once a sailor brought a spotted shell from the Pacific to his sweetheart (some Bet Bouncer of those parts) and put it to her ear, asking her what she heard, and that she answered that it made a noise 'like people coming out of chapel of a Sunday.' Still, there are some ears which, listening in a shell, hear other sounds than that. Leaving the garden of San Carlos, a passing boy turned to his father and asked him who was buried there. The father, who could read and write (*sabia de pluma y de cuentas*), answered him, 'El General Francés.'

El General Francés! So pass fame, honour, and glory, even remembrance. All is vanity, vanity of vanities; all except your gardens by the sea; your gardens wild, neglected, or, at best, cared for by Spanish gardeners, with or without a hero buried in them. These will blossom, do blossom, when the rider and the horse have mouldered into dust, cannons have rusted or been turned to sickles and to horseshoes; and when gallant deeds have been forgotten. At least they blossom to those who, listening in a shell, hear something different to the noise of people leaving a music-hall.

R. B. C. G.

www.ingramcontent.com/pod-product-compliance
Lightning Source LLC
Chambersburg PA
CBHW020111030726
47498CB00006B/2060